The Kiss Bet

wattpad books

An imprint of Wattpad WEBTOON Book Group

Published in Canada by Wattpad WEBTOON Book Group, a division of WEBTOON Entertainment Inc.

36 Wellington Street E., Suite 200, Toronto, ON M5E 1C7 Canada

Published in the United States by Wattpad WEBTOON Book Group, a division of WEBTOON Entertainment Inc.

5700 Wilshire Boulevard, Los Angeles, CA 90036 USA

www.wattpad.com

First Wattpad Books edition: February 2026

ISBN 978-1-99834-174-0 (Trade Paper original)
ISBN 978-1-83411-017-2 (eBook edition)

Library and Archives Canada Cataloguing in Publication information is available upon request.

Printed and bound in Canada

1 3 5 7 9 10 8 6 4 2

Cover design by Lolly Illustrations
Typesetting by Delaney Anderson

The Kiss Bet

FARRAH PENN

BASED ON THE GRAPHIC NOVEL BY
INGRID OCHOA

wattpad books

ONE

SARA

Tonight is the perfect time to begin romanticizing my life.

Why haven't I thought of this sooner? The moon hangs bright and whimsical in the sky, surrounded by glimmering stars. Wood smoke and a hint of cinnamon fill the air, a sign fall is officially here, and I'm so blissfully happy that I could burst like a confetti popper, leaving a thousand shimmering sparkles in my wake. I wouldn't change a thing.

I'm walking to the subway with Vicky and Patrick, who has taken it upon himself to belt the happy birthday song as loudly as his vocal cords will allow. No one asked him to do this, least of all me—the actual birthday girl—but Patrick just carries on like he's on one of those reality singing shows. He prances ahead, in full production mode.

Vicky threads her arm through mine. "How many more times, do you think?"

"*Please,*" I moan. "Let this be the last."

Spoiler alert: it's not. In fact, he's not watching where

he's going and nearly collides with an elderly gentleman, who admonishes him for his volume.

Patrick remains unfazed, jollier than ever. "Sorry, sir. It's my friend's birthday."

"Is it?" the man deadpans. "I couldn't tell."

Once he's out of earshot, I tug Vicky toward the subway entrance. "You're so embarrassing!" I say to Patrick, praying he's not about to start up again.

Lucky for me, he doesn't.

It's late for a school night, but my dad doesn't mind since this is my birthday outing. Plus, I'm with family. Vicky's my cousin, and when Patrick suggested we go to my favorite hot pot place to celebrate, I said we couldn't go without her. Obviously. Most days, Vicky works at Kiki's Chicken Kitchen after school, which is very good, though not as good as hot pot. Anyway, I couldn't have asked for anything better. Except the singing. I can do without the singing.

The three of us pay our fare and navigate through the turnstile. Our train's not due for several minutes, so Vicky and I leisurely descend the steps after Patrick.

"Can you believe you're finally eighteen, Sara Lin?"

"I mean, nothing's changed," I say. "It's just a number."

"I can't believe it." Vicky beams. "It's like you're an adult now!"

"An adult?" Patrick cackles. "Sara Lin still *looks* like a kid. And let's not forget she's never even kissed a boy."

I gasp. "*Patrick*."

He's not wrong. I tell Patrick everything—he's been my best friend for ages—so he'd be the first to know if these lips had had any action. A twist of discomfort tilts in my belly.

Does that make me pathetic? That I'm eighteen now, and haven't had my first kiss yet?

"Well," Vicky says, "it's kinda true. And senior year just started."

Not her too.

I groan. "Stop reminding me."

Vicky only gives me a playful nudge. "You gotta get on it!"

"Excuse me," I say. "It's not like I can control that kind of thing. I just haven't had the opportunity yet, otherwise—"

Otherwise, what? Would I have kissed someone? Surely I would have, except—well. You know in all those romantic films where feelings build between the two leads and then they finally realize they care for each other? There's a whole *moment.* The music swells. They look into each other's eyes. And it's like the whole world stops. Their lips meet and—I don't know—everything just makes sense. It's perfect.

That's what I want my first kiss to feel like.

Patrick swivels around. "So you're saying all you need is an opportunity? And you'll just, what? Do it?" He grins. "I can give you an opportunity right now."

And before I can process what's happening, he moves in close. On the stairs we're now the same height, and his eyes are so blue—an ocean on a clear day kind of blue—and I feel all the blood in my body rush straight into my cheeks, painting my fair skin red, which is an all-too-common occurrence if you're a natural ginger like me. I, unfortunately, can never hide a blush.

"Wh-what do you mean?" I stutter. "That—*you*? You want to just—?"

Is my best friend going to kiss me?

Now? *Here?* On these dirty subway stairs?

But then he bursts out laughing. In my face.

"No way, I'm talking about a *bet*." He raises his eyebrows, all teasing. "Why would you even think that?"

"Clarify next time!" My face will forever be permanently flushed, I just know it. "You're the one who's standing way too close to me."

He backs away, peers around the corner of the platform, then slides back around the wall.

"I have an idea," he says, a mischievous expression forming behind his eyes.

My gaze jumps to Vicky, but she only shrugs. Patrick's antics are a staple in this friendship. I have to admit, it keeps me on my toes.

"I bet you *five bucks*," Patrick begins, all dramatic, "that you won't go up and ask that guy if you can kiss him."

The space between my brows pinches. "What are you—? What guy?"

Patrick chucks a thumb behind him. "That sleeping dude right there."

I peer over his shoulder. A guy our age is sitting on an empty bench, eyes closed, hoodie yanked over his tousled blond hair. He's wearing these browline glasses that are more stylish than nerdy, and he's got a duffel bag slung over his shoulder, like he's headed on a trip. If he goes to our school, I don't recognize him. And I would have. If he did go to Eagle Gate High, that is. Because he's . . . not bad looking. From this distance, anyway.

But—no. Patrick has lost his mind.

"For five bucks? Absolutely not."

Patrick smirks, adjusting his backward cap. "Fine, you

wanna raise the stakes? I'll give you fifty bucks right now if you can get him to kiss you."

My gaze ticks back to the sleeping boy. He looks harmless. And who knows? What if this is my ultimate swoonworthy meet-cute? And on my eighteenth birthday! Doesn't everyone want a *Sixteen Candles* moment? Sure, I'm two years late, but who cares?

Destiny is in my hands. I'll gather up the nerve to go over and ask if he'll kiss me, and then he'll look into my eyes like he's never seen anyone on this earthly plane who possesses more beauty than the girl standing before him. We'll kiss, fall in love, and whenever anyone asks how we met, he'll chuckle and say, *It was so sweet! If Sara hadn't had the guts to kiss me, who knows what would have happened?*

But *do I* have the guts to do all that?

Patrick cocks a brow. "I knew you couldn't—"

Before he can even finish his sentence, I whirl on my heel and march toward the boy.

My heartbeat thuds rapidly in my chest as I pause in front of him. He's still asleep. Heat blooms up my neck and into my cheeks. I'm grateful there's no reflective surfaces around, because I'm *positive* I resemble an overripe strawberry. It feels like I've arrived at the top of a roller coaster, anticipating the moment when my stomach flips like a pancake and adrenaline races down my spine.

My gaze drops to the floor. Wait! We're wearing matching Sambas, white with burgundy stripes. What are the odds? That has to mean something, right? Matching shoes equals . . . soulmates? Either way, this is absolutely meet-cute material.

I take one itty-bitty step closer. The thudding in my chest accelerates and—what am I *thinking*? I can't do this!

As I'm turning away, I spot Patrick and Vicky watching me with rapt anticipation. Patrick whisper-yells, "You're gonna lose, chicken!" while Vicky clasps her hands and mouths, *You can do it, Sara!*

I pull a deep breath into my lungs. There's no way I'm losing Patrick's bet. I'm not going to let him think I'm some coward who can't even approach a boy. I'd never live that down. Vicky's right—I *got* this. I'll just wake him up. That's not hard, is it? Step one: wake him up. Step two—

Well, we'll get there.

I face him again. Golden strands of hair fall around his face, which is a very nice face. I haven't spent much time admiring boy bone structure, but maybe I should. That could become my new hobby. Appreciating a good face. He's got an angular jaw, thick eyebrows, and soft-looking skin. Headphones cover his ears—which I hadn't noticed before, since his hoodie's partially obstructing them—and I wonder what he's listening to.

He's kind of cute.

Okay, I can do this. I'm the one who wanted to romanticize my life, and isn't this one way to do it?

I crouch a tiny bit, leveling myself with the bench, and move closer. I'm just going to tap him on the shoulder and—

VOOOSH.

A huge gust of wind barrels along the platform as our train rushes forward, all speed-fueled momentum, wheels rumbling along the steel line.

Oh no. No, no, no, no—

The boy opens his eyes. And stares right at me.

Do not panic. This is it! If I don't ask him now, I really am a coward. I mean, I'm a whole year older now. I *have* to start taking chances. Embrace my destiny! And besides, if I chicken out, I'll always wonder if this could have been the meet-cute of my dreams. What if this is the beginning of something really spectacular? Am I gonna let that slip by?

So I swallow, gather the courage, and then say, "Can I kiss you?"

TWO

PATRICK

You know, I didn't think Sara had the guts to *actually* do it.

THREE

SARA

New rule. Romanticizing my life? Taking risks? Terrible idea. Horrible. Geez, who put me in charge of these decisions? (Okay, yes. I did. But *still.*) But if Patrick hadn't baited me with that bet—

"You know," Dad says, interrupting my thought spiral, "you've been washing that same dish for the last five minutes."

Glancing down, I discover that I have, in fact, been scrubbing my breakfast plate with so much gusto you'd think it'd personally wronged me. Lost in my own head once again. Typical. But who can blame me? I've spent all morning playing back my enormous Kiss A Stranger fumble in agonizing detail, rewinding those excruciating moments like a slow-motion replay.

Allow me to set the scene. I approach cute Subwayboy, heart ablaze, ready for my love life to *finally* change. His eyes open—moss-green eyes, I notice—and right after I ask if I can kiss him, he immediately jerks back like I am a five-foot tap-dancing cockroach come to lure him to my underground lair. Irritation flits across his face. He yanks off his headphones, and the first words he says to me aren't *Wow, you're so beautiful! Yes, of course I'll kiss you!* but *Excuse me?!*

That's right. *Excuse me?!*

Well, ladies and gentlemen, I guess that's a no.

Then he has the audacity to glare, eyes darting around. "What the heck? Is this a prank—for the internet or something?" He crosses his arms. "Because hell no, I'm not kissing you. For all I know, you're some weirdo."

Think that's bad? Trust me, it gets worse.

My mouth transforms into the Sahara Desert. I have no idea what to say. Words? What are those? All the while my mind is screaming *Run! RUN!* And as I go to take a step back, my feet tangle with his. Before I can grasp what's happening, I trip, my palms catch the floor before my face smacks the ground, and a hot flush crashes over me like a tidal wave.

Of course this would happen to me.

A light *thump* sounds as my dad sets down his coffee, yanking me back to reality.

"And," he continues, "it's already seven fifteen. You're going to be late for school."

"What? Why didn't you say?" I cease scrubbing and shut off the tap, drying my hands on a rag before rushing to the kitchen table to grab my shoulder bag.

"I did say," he counters as I'm pulling on my shoes. "Have fun, make good choices, and, most importantly, make sure you tell your friends how cool your dad is."

Making a conscious effort to not roll my eyes, I blow him a half-hearted kiss as I exit. I've barely pulled the door closed behind me when a presence sidles up beside me and says, "Good *morning*, Sara!"

My hand leaps to my chest, heart rate working overtime. But it's only Patrick, which is weird, because Patrick doesn't live in my apartment building.

He's leaning against the wall, one leg crossed over the other, the poster child of *casual.* Except there's a wicked smirk on his face, like he's very much up to something.

"You scared me." I adjust my shoulder strap. "What are you doing here?"

His blue eyes flash playfully. "I'm an early bird, what can I say?"

I stare at him, waiting for the real answer.

"Fine, I came to pick you up."

My brows knit in confusion. "You never do that."

Suddenly, the door across the hall opens and Mr. Yang steps out, briefcase in hand, wearing his usual work slacks and navy sweater.

"Oh—morning, Mr. Yang!" I say, a cheerful lilt in my voice.

Mr. Yang smiles, bowing his head sightly before walking to the stairs.

I'm familiar with almost all our neighbors since Dad and I have lived in this apartment building for a while. Mr. Yang is quiet, kind, and somewhat elusive. He doesn't have kids and will sometimes talk to Dad about old-school rock music—or yacht rock, as I call it—though you'll never catch me admitting it's grown on me. I often hum Queen under my breath while studying, and Patrick always tells me to knock it off.

Patrick snaps his fingers overdramatically. "Oh! You know

what? Now that I'm here, you might as well pay me for last night's bet!"

Panic zips up my spine. "*Patrick.* Don't talk about that in front of people." I nod toward Mr. Yang's retreating figure, lowering my voice. "That's the real reason you're here, isn't it? You punk."

He cackles, eyes gleaming, and I take this as an opportunity to race toward the elevator like I'm fleeing a crime scene.

Patrick's footsteps fall behind me. "Hey, wait up! What about the money?"

I increase my pace, slyly ignoring the last part. "*What?* I can't hear you. Hurry up, we're going to be late!"

Dad gave me fifty bucks for my birthday. It's all I have, so the last thing I want is to give any of it to Patrick. That schemer. Maybe he'll forget, take pity on my embarrassing moment, and realize I've already lost my dignity—I don't need to lose my money too.

FOUR

PATRICK

A bet's a bet. If Sara thinks I'll forget about the money, she's wrong. And outrunning me won't stop me from nagging her about it!

FIVE
SARA

As Mr. Day drones on about fractal curves, all I can think about is how *fractal* sounds like *pterodactyl*. Then I try to remember how to spell *pterodactyl* in the corner of my notebook. It definitely starts with a *p* and—ugh. I should pay attention. How is calculus a requirement to graduate? It's so *boring*. I might perish from boredom. In fact, I might become the first girl to *ever* perish from a mind-numbing calculus lesson, and that will forever be my legacy. Here lies Sara Lin, bored to death by fractal curves.

Eagle Gate High isn't bad overall. There are around one hundred students total in my senior class and, for the most part, everyone is nice. Except Rose, who—much like her name suggests—has some thorns alongside her sweetness.

It's funny, because this place felt so *gargantuan* when I started as a freshman. Eagle Gate is a red brick building with multiple floors and stairways, but it's not so bad once you know where you're going. (Once I came back from the bathroom and walked into the wrong classroom, which was mortifying, but not as mortifying as my encounter with Subwayboy yesterday.) There are huge windows in every classroom that invite in natural light, and I always try to sit near one so I can pretend I'm outside whenever my mind wanders. Which is pretty frequently, especially in calculus.

Will I *ever* use this stuff in the real world?

"*Psst*, Sara Lin."

Glancing to my left, I lock eyes with Tammy Yokoyama. She's this sweet, shy girl who wears these oversized retro glasses every day. We met our first year here in English and have been friendly ever since, sometimes eating lunch together and talking in depth about our favorite K-pop idols.

"I heard you almost had your first kiss last night."

"*Tammy*." I'm horrified. "Why would you bring that up right now?"

"Because I'm bored," she whispers. "And, hey. It's your first rejection. Did he really call you a weirdo?"

From the desk directly behind her, Patrick snickers.

I lean in, voice low. "Oh my god, Tammy, how do you even know about—?"

She grins. "Patrick told me."

Of course.

Rose—who's sitting right in front of Tammy—whirls around to face me, scowling. "Be quiet, Sara Lin. No one cares about your kissing. I can't focus."

Rose does not bother to whisper this, because why would she? Eyes from all over the room tick over to me. I flush. Ugh. Can she keep her voice *down*? People listen to and respect Rose. She's a natural leader, which is why she's president of

Newspaper Club, but she was also blessed with looking like a CoverGirl model. I mean, long blond hair? Perfect skin? Flawless smile? Why do some people have it all? *And* she's smart. Like, ten times better at calculus than me.

Mr. Day turns from the chalkboard, his attention now on me. "Sara, are you talking during my lecture again?"

Ah! What did I do to deserve this? I'm not the one who started this conversation in the first place!

"I—" I begin.

"No more talking." He's already facing the board, chalk tapping as he writes. "Why don't you see me after class?"

A hot blush creeps into my cheeks. Rose seems satisfied as she resumes taking notes, and I'm forced to stew in my own dread until the bell rings, whereupon I stay seated while everyone else gathers their belongings and exits. At least Patrick gives me a tiny *yikes, sorry* shrug on his way out.

As soon as the last student leaves, Mr. Day turns to me. "Sara, are you aware of your grade in this class?"

Oh, am I aware that I've been marked so low on my last few quizzes I've probably offended Sir Isaac Newton from beyond the grave? Unfortunately, yes.

I swallow, my stomach already in knots. "I'm aware."

"So you know you're failing calculus." He opens his grade book and slides his finger to my name. "I know it's early on in the year, but it's not looking good. I don't want you to fall behind."

Mr. Day teaches all the core subjects to our senior class, which means he's aware I *can* fall behind if I don't get it together. The worst part is, I try to study hard. Sure, *maybe* I get distracted texting Patrick or checking Instagram or scrolling through celebrity news or updating my blog—but I'm only human. I've given my all to Mr. Day's calculus quizzes and, somehow, I've ended up doing terribly every time.

"The information tends to go over my head," I admit. "It's always been hard for me. I'm not great at math."

"Well, I want you to succeed. And I'm sure your father would appreciate that, too, so I'm going to recommend a student tutor for you." He pulls out a folder and searches through it. "You'll meet after school. That is, if you have some time next week?"

"Yeah," I say warily. "Okay."

He shuffles through his paperwork until he finds what he's looking for. "A-ha—right. Oliver. He's a new student here, but he comes with excellent recommendations."

I'm nodding politely even as my confidence sinks below sea level. "Sounds good."

Mr. Day smiles, peering at me above his bifocals. "I've had plenty of students struggle with calculus, Sara. You're not alone. Extra tutoring can help."

I tell him I'll work harder and try to focus better, but inside, my tenacity shrivels like a deflating balloon. If I can't kiss a cute boy without it blowing up in my face—and if I can't pass calculus—is there *anything* I can do well? Confidence and grace and intelligence come so easily to people like Rose. Meanwhile, I'm struggling.

What is wrong with me? Am I really destined to begin my eighteenth year as a gigantic failure?

Oh god, anything but that.

SIX

SARA

Later, as I'm walking home from school, I make the mistake of calling my dad as he's heading home from the office.

My dad's an accountant. I know, believe me, the irony is not lost on me. Sometimes during dinner he'll randomly decide I need a lesson in 1040 tax forms and, oh, wouldn't it be so fun to learn about accounts payable and accounts receivable? Um, no, Dad. Allow me to fill you in on Beyoncé instead.

But I'd rather not get a lecture from him at the dinner table tonight, so why not rip the bandage off with a phone call?

"Am I going to have to start restricting outings if you can't focus on your grades?" he's saying. "I can't believe this!"

"Dad," I whine. "I already told you—I got a tutor. Everything's going to be okay!"

In between leaving Mr. Day's classroom and starting this walk home, I decided I gave up on the romanticizing thing too soon. Tammy was right. It was my first rejection! So what? Am I going to let a silly boy's opinion stop me from living my best life? Who the heck cares about what some random thinks about me, anyway?

Clearly Subwayboy was *not* the right boy. He's probably a terrible kisser, which means there's someone better out there for me. Someone taller, cuter—*wiser*.

Besides, in all those classic rom-coms, the main character gets to know someone, starts falling for them, and *then* experiences a magical, out-of-body kiss that changes their life. And that's what I really want. I can't just skip ahead to the kissing part! I have to complete the *knowing* part—the *love* part. It's integral. This makes the kiss *mean* something.

"Please take tutoring seriously, Sara. Don't get distracted now—it's your senior year." He sighs, and I hear the concern in his tone. He's probably wondering why I'm not more like Vicky. Vicky's great at math—and a great, wonderful human in general. "Are you on your way home?"

"Almost there," I say, the worry already creeping back in. Am I too daydreamy? Ugh, he might be right. "See you soon."

Once we hang up, it's like a storm cloud looms over me. I can't believe I have a tutor. Why can't calculus click for me like it does for everyone else? This stinks. I freaking hate school—well, the hard parts, anyway—and now I have to do *more* school *after* school?

I could cry.

Actually—no. I don't want to cry in public. That isn't a good way to romanticize. Besides, there's a guy from school walking ahead of me, backpack slung over his shoulders. The last thing I need is for him to see me bawling my eyes out, then tell the whole school that I'm some crying weirdo who's bad at math. I'll save the waterworks for when I'm in my room, *thank you very much*. It's the least I can do to repair my dignity.

My gaze drops and—wait a second. Those shoes. The Sambas from yesterday. The hoodie tugged over his head!

It's not him, is it? I mean, plenty of people have those shoes. Including me.

But then he turns his head just slightly, glancing to the right, and now I can see he's on the phone.

"Yeah, I know—" he's saying.

Oh no. It *is* him.

Subwayboy.

This cannot be happening to me.

So I do the first thing that pops into my bad-at-math brain: I veer aside and jump into an overgrown evergreen shrub.

Twigs snap and crack, and brush tangles in my hair as I duck out of sight. I crouch low as I peer through the leaves. Subwayboy pauses. Did he hear me? Please, *please* say no. I can't handle this on top of everything else right now.

But no. He only glances around, then resumes walking.

What the ever-loving heck is he doing here? I was never supposed to see him again! In fact, as Patrick, Vicky, and I sprinted onto the oncoming train and the doors closed, leaving him in the dust, I thought, *Whew! At least we didn't continue this awkward encounter in the same car!* I even pressed my forehead against the window, watching him grow smaller and smaller as we took off, thinking, *Goodbye, forever, Subwayboy with good taste in shoes!*

Ha-ha-ha, do you hear that sarcastic laughter? Because my life is one gigantic joke. Subwayboy is here, in my neighborhood, and he's—

No. You are kidding me.

He's walking into my building.

Tell me I'm hallucinating. This isn't real life. As I leap from my hidden position in the bush, dusting dirt and leaves from my uniform skirt, I get a better look. Yep. He's definitely heading into my building.

I dart after him, because *what* is going on? Did he find out where I live? Is he coming to confront me in person? No, there's no way—right?

The automatic doors slide open as I grow closer. That's when I see he's already entering the elevator.

No chance am I pressing the button and risking the elevator doors opening too soon, guaranteeing a face-to-face encounter. (See? Maybe I am smart.) So instead I race to the stairwell and take the steps two at a time. This building is enormous. There's no way I'll run into him again, but I can't risk it. All I have to do is get to my floor as fast as I can, dash to my door, unlock it, and hide inside forever and ever.

Seems reasonable enough.

Right as I'm pushing the stairwell door open, the elevator down the hall lets out an idyllic *ding!* My pulse trips. I hop back into the stairwell and tug the door partially closed, peeking through the crack.

Agh, no!

Subwayboy exits the elevator and starts down the hallway, using a key to unlock the door to apartment forty-one. Then he disappears inside, the door slamming behind him.

This is not ideal, seeing as the unit he just entered is *right* across from my apartment.

I slap my palm against forehead and inwardly cringe. Subwayboy lives directly across the hall.

Why me?

SEVEN

SARA

As it turns out, I did not lock myself in my apartment forever because Dad wouldn't allow it, which is rude, considering my list of problems is currently out of control.

When he asked me why I felt the need to hide inside all weekend, I couldn't tell him the truth. I mean, ME? Telling *my dad* about the kiss bet and Subwayboy? I'd rather give up hot pot for an entire year than hear what he'd have to say about that. Some things aren't meant for Dad ears.

Anyway, at that point, I made chamomile tea, put on a cozy sweater, and then vented the entire story to my blog, which I found highly cathartic.

Nobody aside from Patrick and Vicky knows about my blog, which is fine. I don't write for views or anything. It's more of an outlet. A way for me to express my feelings—and I have *a ton* of feelings.

If I'm honest, I think I'm a decent writer. My words have a certain flair, and the more I write, the better I get. That's what

Vicky says, anyway, because she stopped by with food from Kiki's Chicken Kitchen after she read my latest post.

"You have to leave the house eventually, Sara," she told me before she left. "It might even be good for you to run into Subwayboy."

Good for me? In what universe would that be good for me? I don't even know what I'd say to him.

No, it's best to remain cowardly and avoid him until I come up with a better solution.

Now it's Monday, and I'm walking into calculus class when I catch several students removing a paper from their folders. My stomach drops. The homework! I forgot to do it over the weekend. This is not a great look for me, especially after my conversation with Mr. Day on Friday. I've got to try harder.

The bell hasn't rung yet. Maybe I can salvage this.

I slink back to Patrick's desk, hoping I go unnoticed by Mr. Day. "Hey, did you do the homework?"

Patrick looks up, his features displaying cunning indifference. "Are you saying you were home all weekend and didn't even do the assignment?"

"I was, uh—busy!" I grab his worksheet. "Let me copy just this once."

He tugs his paper from my hands. "That's gonna be fifty bucks. Because you still owe me, remember?"

This stupid kiss bet is ruining my life.

I tuck my hair behind my ear. "Are you kidding me?"

He only raises his brows. "Wanna make it seventy-five?"

I slap my fifty on his desk, defeated. Because what choice do I have? This is my own fault, and I can't let my calculus grade get any lower.

"It's all I have," I say.

Patrick pockets the bill then lets me have his worksheet. "I should really start my own business, don't you think?"

I'm already back at my desk, furiously scribbling answers as fast as my hand will allow.

"Please," I intone, not bothering to glance back at him. "Shut up."

"*Hmm.*" The sound is overexaggerated as he drags his chair beside my desk. "Who can I bet you to kiss next?"

I jab his side with my elbow. "Will you quit talking about that? Can't you see it's a sensitive topic?"

Patrick's teasing isn't anything new. In fact, it's his preferred method of communication within our best-friend dynamic. That's just who he is, and I don't mind—because I serve it right back. I've got my own comeback arsenal. And besides, we're never cruel to each other. We keep it playful.

My hand cramps but I don't let it stop me. I can do this. Only a few seconds left until class starts. Mr. Day will never know I blanked on the assignment.

"Okay, class, eyes up here," Mr. Day announces.

I don't bother following those directions, because I'm *almost* finished. So! Close!

"We have a new student, so I want you all to warmly welcome him to class," Mr. Day continues. "Would you like to introduce yourself?"

It's at this moment everything comes to a record-scratching halt. I freeze, still hunched over the equations, and squeeze my eyes shut. I already know what will happen when I open them—it's *just* my luck. The new student is Subwayboy. I'm so certain that I'm willing to place another bet with Patrick.

This *would* happen to me. Now I'm going to have to see him every single day in calculus class.

My gaze flicks to the front of the room and—oh.

Whew.

It's not Subwayboy.

But *oh my gosh.* This boy has a dazzling smile, the kind that sets your soul aglow. His green eyes scan the new faces before him, but he doesn't seem intimidated or shy. He's totally comfortable, really. If I was starting a new school my senior year, I'd be terrified. He only radiates outward friendliness—like a golden retriever.

His grin widens. "Hi, I'm Joseph! But please just call me Joe."

Joe. He's so cute. I can't stop staring, heart thrumming like tiny hummingbird wings. He's got a swoop of jet-black hair with stray pieces falling effortlessly over his forehead. And—wow. He's tall. Extremely attractive. So much so that my eyes might have morphed into hearts.

Mr. Day picks up his chalk. "Go ahead and take a seat, Joe."

Joe starts down the aisle, heading my way. Because the only empty desk is in front of me.

My breath catches in my throat. As he grows closer, our gazes tangle. Oh my. Two dimples frame his adorable smile, and the warm sunlight streaming through the window enhances his forest-green eyes. My world slows. From the way he's looking at me, it's like I'm the only person in the room.

His hand moves to scoot out his chair, and then he says, "Hi."

He's saying hi! To *me.*

Say something, Sara!

"Hi," I manage.

He slides his backpack off his shoulders and sits, turning his attention to Mr. Day. I'm not sure how long I've been staring at the back of his beautiful hair when a wad of paper hits my temple.

My infatuation haze lifts. When I blink back to reality, I peer around and find all the girls are *also* staring at Joe.

Oh—well, then. It's not just me who's entranced by his appeal.

As I whirl around to figure out where that paper came from, Patrick glowers at me, aim poised to throw another paper wad. He looks more annoyed than usual, mouth twisted in a deep grimace.

He points at my desk. "Gimme back my homework."

EIGHT

PATRICK

I don't get it. The new guy isn't even *that* good-looking. I don't see the big whatzeedo about him—and why is Sara suddenly so enamored, anyway?

NINE
SARA

When school ends, I skip out the double doors with Patrick and Tammy, ready to embrace my sweet, sweet freedom, before I remember—oh, right. Tutoring. I can't escape yet.

Ugh.

This doesn't bode well for me. Honestly? I tried to make an effort in calculus today, but then Joe happened. Instead of paying attention to Mr. Day, I found myself entranced by Joe's beautiful hair. How silky it seemed—and then I imagined running my fingers through it. A harmless daydream, really.

But get this: Mr. Day had us pass new worksheets to the person behind us, and Joe's fingers brushed mine when he handed me the stack. I swear, the briefest touch sent a jolt of electricity down my arm. And then he smiled again—at *me*—and swept some hair away from his stunning green eyes before turning back to face the front.

"Sara? Did you hear what I said?"

I blink away the Joe haze. Patrick and Tammy have started

walking ahead of me, and now they're glancing back to see if I'm going to catch up. Meanwhile, I'm stalled at the top of the steps with my head in the clouds.

I adjust my cozy plaid scarf around my neck. "Sorry, what?"

"I said, are you coming to karaoke?" Patrick repeats.

There's this karaoke spot we found a year or so ago on our walk home, but the best part? It's cheap. Fifteen bucks and you can have a room for an hour. We're not great singers, but it doesn't matter. We have fun combing through the gigantic songbook and picking out surprise musical numbers for each other, and after, we'll usually stop in for hot pot.

"Ah, I forgot—I can't. I have tutoring, remember?"

"Aw, come on! Tammy's going"—he slings an arm around her shoulders—"and she never comes to anything. Just reschedule."

Agh, it's so tempting. Dad will never know if I skip this once, right?

No. Best not to risk it. I'll totally get grounded if he finds out.

"I can't." I begin retracing my steps. "Sorry, have fun, though! I'll see you tomorrow!"

Spinning on my heel, I reach for the door and head inside before I can clock the disappointment on Patrick's face.

Almost everyone has left for the day. The halls aren't bustling with activity. The corridor walls are speckled with handmade posters promoting school activities. JOIN TRACK AND FIELD, one reads. Uh, no thanks. I'm not much of an athlete. Another says, EAGLE GATE SCHOOL FESTIVAL SEPTEMBER 15TH! REMEMBER TO SIGN YOUR CLUB UP FOR A BOOTH!

As I make my way to the library, I unearth the paper Mr. Day gave me last week. *Oliver Yang, Library Room 12-B.* There's a contact number printed underneath.

I'm familiar with the library. We come during English class sometimes to find reference texts, which are a bit dry, but I could get lost in the fiction section all day. Reading is sort of like daydreaming—the way you get lost in a story—and I love that feeling. I think it's partly why I like writing my blog so much.

As I reach the library door, ready to push my way in, I freeze when my eyes land on a familiar face through the window. Because there, sitting at a study table, is none other than Subwayboy.

I gasp and flatten my back against the wall so he won't spot me if he glances up. No! Why do I keep running into this guy? Maybe I'm in the wrong room, so I check the information again. *Room 12-B, Library.* This is it. He's currently the only one inside, so that must mean he's my tutor.

Or—maybe not? What if that is *not* Oliver Yang, because Oliver Yang is running late? Yes, I'm sure that's it.

There's only one way to find out, so I whip out my phone and text the contact number.

Sara: Hi, this is Sara Lin. Are we still meeting in room 12-B?

I tilt my head ever so slightly, eyes on him as he glances at his phone. He picks it up, types, then sets it back face down. A second later, my phone buzzes. I scan the message, heart sinking.

Unknown Number: Yep. I'm here already. See you soon

It *is* him. Subwayboy has a name. Oliver Yang. Oliver Yang, my calculus tutor.

What did I do to deserve this? And more importantly, what the heck do I do now? I don't have time to text Patrick and ask for advice. Besides, he's half the reason I'm in this mess. Vicky would know what to do, but she's already started her shift at Kiki's and won't have access to her phone.

Okay—*think*. Hadn't I been brave enough to ask him to kiss me? If I could do that, surely I can channel that same courage right now. All I have to do is march in there and face the consequences head-on. If he recognizes me, so what? It's a chance to clear the air, isn't it?

I spare another peek. He's got his chunky headphones over his ears again, just like when I spotted him at the station, soft golden hair sticking out in every direction. His eyes are focused on writing something down, pen scribbling, looking lost in whatever he's doing. It reminds me of, well, *me* when I'm typing out a blog post. Like the entire world around you disappears and it's only you and your writing.

Here's my opportunity to start fresh. To prove I'm a different person this year. Someone bold—confident. Determined. So I take a deep breath and—

Completely wimp out.

My scarf is a handy disguise, it turns out, and I use it to cover my nose and mouth while tugging my short hair into a bun that sprouts like a flower from my head. I've got a few spare bobby pins in my shoulder bag, so I clip my bangs back before fishing my round glasses from their case and sliding them on. There! No way he'll recognize me now.

Then, after taking a deep breath, I enter the library.

I'm looming over his table when he looks up at me, pen paused mid-sentence. He yanks his headphones from his ears and lets them fall around his neck, confusion settling in his pinched brows.

"Uh," he starts. "You're Sara?"

"Mm-hmm!" The sound comes out muffled from behind my scarf.

He sets his headphones on the desk beside him as I slip into the chair, tugging my shoulder bag to my chest like it's a safety blanket. This is clearly odd behavior—I can see it on his face—but he doesn't bring it up. Instead, he draws his calculus book closer.

"All right, then." His gaze flicks to me. "What chapters are on your next test?"

Instead of answering like a normal person, I hold up my two pointer fingers.

He stares at me, unamused. "Eleven?"

I nod vigorously. See? This wasn't my worst idea!

"Okay, so, sequences and series." Oliver flips to the correct page. "I want you to explain what you already understand."

Uh-oh. This is a problem. First, because I understand very little. And second, I did not expect to do much talking here. He's the tutor, after all. I'm supposed to soak in the information in silent concentration. He speaks, I listen. Isn't that the point?

Oliver's mouth flattens, eyes narrowing as he waits for me to answer. I've got to give him *something*.

"Mm, mmfh fuhm? Mm fuhum mh—"

Is my scarf limiting my enunciation? Sure. Do I care? Absolutely not.

But what *is* crystal clear is the fact he's annoyed.

"*What?*" He sighs, aggravated, and uses his pointer fingers to pinch the bridge of his nose. His glasses rise like an elevator as he does this, tangling with his floppy bangs. When he lowers his hands, he's fully glaring at me. "Will you pull that down? I can't understand a word you're saying."

Before I can stop him, he reaches over and tugs down my scarf.

Heat blooms in my face as my jaw slackens in shock—*did he figure me out?!*—but he just stares into my soul with what I'm now realizing is his signature unamused expression. One eyebrow raised, mouth tilted down. All business without an ounce of friendliness, and this makes me I wonder if he's ever experienced real human joy. Maybe he should try karaoke.

"You were saying?" he prompts.

Confirmation: He doesn't recognize me.

Phew.

"Um," I start. "Sequences? Are those the, uh, numbers? With the letters?"

Oliver hangs his head, disappointment evident. "Let's just start from the beginning."

Well, great. He assumes that I possess one single brain cell. Not even that—perhaps he believes there's a wet noodle floating around in there instead of a brain.

My blush deepens, but he's already turning his textbook toward me.

"Sequences are numbers that follow a pattern in a specific order, which are either infinite or finite," he explains in this monotonous, dull tone. Geez, he's worse than Mr. Day. "And a series is the sum of the terms in a sequence, then you have numbers in a sequence. Those are called *terms*. So you see here, *n* is your index variable. Now, we can denote this infinite ordered list by—"

My brain pulses. (Because, yes, I do have one.) A headache starts to form behind my eyes, and my vision goes all glossy and ethereal. I *swear* I'm trying to focus, but he's regurgitating what's printed in the textbook like reading comprehension is my biggest issue. This doesn't make the math magically click.

He goes on for the next hour. Any time he asks "Make sense?" I only nod, even though I'm retaining very little. My eyes keep ticking to the clock on the wall, begging for time to speed up. I'm *exhausted.* Who knew calculus could zap all your energy?

"Okay, complete those worksheets since that's your homework, and then we'll review it next time we meet." He closes his textbook. "When's your first test?"

"Next week," I tell him. "I've bombed my quizzes so far."

"Right." He's already on his feet, slinging his headphones around his neck before packing his textbook in his backpack. "Then let's start meeting every day after school."

Every. Day?!

"Okay," I mutter, because what else can I do but agree to this torture? I have to pass this class.

"Great." He barely glances at me as he strides toward the door. "Bye."

What's his deal? It's like he's allergic to pleasantry and kindness. Do I smell or something? I sniff my armpits. Nope, I'm as sweet as a peach. Then what is it? This weird disguise?

Ugh—I guess it doesn't matter now. He's finally gone, which means I can let out the tight breath that's wound around my lungs. Sweet air! Sweet relief!

That was pure emotional agony, and now I'm going to have to endure it every single day. I could cry. Why would I agree?

Oh, right. Because I can't fail this class. If I do, Dad will make sure I never have a social life ever again, which means I'll never see Vicky or Patrick or do fun things like karaoke or meet a boy who might fall for me.

On the one hand, getting grounded from social activities means I won't run into Subwayboy Oliver when I'm coming and going from my building. But on the other hand, I can't exactly go on romanticizing my life if I'm stuck in my room. And isn't that the whole idea? I need to put myself out there more. To embrace romance and whimsy! To be vulnerable and try new things!

That's settled, then. He lives across from me, so I'm going to have to risk running into him, but I'll keep our interactions strictly limited to the library, while wearing my disguise.

I can't confront him about the subway. Maybe that makes me a chicken, but I don't want to rehash that embarrassing moment ever again. It's bad enough Tammy brought it up in class.

So it's settled. Oliver Yang will never, *ever* know I was Subwaygirl.

TEN

PATRICK

"Slow down." I smash my phone to my ear while covering my other one with my hand to drown out the street noise. "You did *what* with the scarf?"

"I wrapped it around my face, of course, but then he goes and freaking pulls it down!"

Sara's been my best friend since we started at Eagle Gate four years ago, so I'm used to her blustery panic. I like that I'm the first person she calls or texts when she needs to vent. It makes me feel important. Plus, she's given me access to her blog, where she documents her encounters in this funny, relatable way. Her writing makes me laugh out loud sometimes, and she knows there's nothing I love more than a good laugh. I joke around a lot and can be super-unserious, but Sara is someone I trust with my own problems too. It's why we're so close.

Sara doesn't live that far from me, so I started walking to her building as soon as I heard the stress in her tone.

The truth is, I missed her at karaoke earlier. She always picks the most random songs—I honestly never know what to expect—and that's half the fun. Tammy's cool, but she chooses these long power ballads that put me to sleep. Sara's good at getting Tammy to pick something more upbeat, so this tutoring thing is already getting in the way.

I pause at a crosswalk, waiting for traffic to clear. "Are you serious?"

"Yes, Patrick! I *seriously* almost fainted!"

"That's hilarious." The intersection clears, and I dart across. "So you think he remembers you, then?"

"I guess not." A crinkle, then a crunch. I'd bet a hundred bucks she's eating cheese puffs, but I doubt she'd take me up on *another* bet. "He calls me a weirdo, and, sure, I'm bad at calculus, but at least I'm not stupid enough to not recognize someone I've seen before."

I sidestep a puddle. "Feisty, Sara Lin."

"*Agh*, you're right. I shouldn't say that about him. It's mean." She sighs. "Gah! I still can't believe I asked if I could kiss him. I'm so embarrassed."

"Calm down." I've reached the final intersection. The crossing signal ushers me forward, so I sprint across the street and slide through her building's double doors. Fragrant lemongrass hits my nostrils when I step into the lobby, a scent I've come to associate with her over time. I've been here a lot. "I bet he doesn't even remember that was you."

"You think so?"

I take the stairs two at a time because I don't want to risk losing service in the elevator. "Yeah, he would've said something by now, right?"

"I guess so."

"Yeah, he would have. For sure." I push open the stairwell door and saunter down her hall, pausing when I'm near her front door. "Hey, I'm kinda hungry. You hungry?"

"Are you kidding? I'm *starving*." Her tone brightens. "Hot pot? But—*ugh*, I don't even want to go outside in case I run into him."

I glance around. Empty. "Nah, no worries. The coast is clear."

"What? Oh!" On the other end, I hear her scrambling. She must have accidentally stepped on the cheese puff bag, but she seems unbothered. There's elation in her voice. "Are you outside? What the heck, Patrick!"

Before I can confirm, she flings open the front door.

I grin. "Surprise."

We hang up our phones. She's wearing a striped pink shirt that matches the scrunchie in her hair, which is half up, half down. Sara cut her hair before senior year because she wanted a sophisticated and chic look, something that made her look older and wiser and less like a child. It worked, if you ask me. She got bangs, too, except she's always pinning them back so they're out of her face.

Her eyes dance with excitement. "Hot pot?"

"*Fine*." I'm only acting like I'm bothered. I love hot pot. "I'll let you choose tonight's meal even though it's my money. My treat, after all."

She tugs a lavender sweater over her head then slips into her sneakers. "Hey, I'm the one who gave you all that money, you dork."

I laugh. "You didn't give me *this* much."

I reach into my pocket and then theatrically display an array of twenties.

"Yeah, I did, Patrick." She closes the door behind her, locking it with her key. "Even more than that, actually."

"Nuh-uh, just look"—I wave the money in her face—"at all these bills."

She playfully swats me away. "You already spent half of it, didn't you?"

"I'll never tell."

It's clear she doesn't want to wait around for the elevator and risk running into Subwayboy, so we take the stairs.

Sara's smart—really, she is—it's just calculus that doesn't stick. And she's already had a hard day. Nobody wants to hang at school longer than they have to, so she deserves this. Yeah, most of it *is* her money, but her cash has brought us together now, if you think about it, and that's what really counts.

When she grins up at me, an enthusiastic skip in her step, I know this was a good idea. It's senior year, she's my best friend, and we're as inseparable as ever.

I'd bet anything that isn't going to change.

ELEVEN

SARA

My eyes are heavy at breakfast the next morning, a general tiredness hanging in my bones. How is it only Tuesday? The week just started and it already feels never-ending.

I'm taking a bite of toast when Dad peers over his coffee, studying me. A crinkle of dissatisfaction deepens across his forehead. He was at the office late last night—which isn't shocking, considering he often works long hours. I'm never sure how he manages to summon enough energy in the mornings after crunching numbers for so long.

It's a shame I didn't inherit his mathematics capabilities. If I had, I wouldn't have to go to calculus tutoring with Subwayboy.

"When did you go to bed last night?"

"Huh?" I take a bite, toast crumbles falling on my skirt. I brush them away. "Sure."

He uses his thumb and forefinger to pinch his forehead, like I'm giving him a headache. "That's not what I asked. Were you out late with that boy Patrick again?"

My eyes jump to his. I set down my toast. "Hm?"

"You know I don't like you hanging out with him so much."

"*Daaad*," I groan. Ugh, he's so overprotective sometimes. "It's fine. We were just eating dinner."

"What happened to all those girlfriends you used to have at school?" He sets his coffee on the table. "Jane, Tammy—oh! Bon Bon?"

I snort. "Who the heck's Bon Bon?"

"You know, the little magician girl!"

"Who, *Lulu*?" For the record, Lulu's into tarot and palm readings, not amateur magic tricks. "Dad, that wasn't even close!"

"Well, whatever." He scoops some eggs onto his fork. "I think you can do so much better than Patrick as a boyfriend. I'm just saying."

"Dad?! What the heck, I'm not dating Patrick." I resist the urge to smack my forehead. How many times have I told him this? "Besides, I already know he's not interested, okay?"

"How do you know that?"

I drop my gaze to my plate. "He said so himself."

I remember his exact words. *Um, how do I say this? Sorry, Sara. I don't feel the same.*

That happened a year ago, toward the end of junior year. The embarrassment could've eaten me alive, but Patrick didn't let it. Instead, we pretended I'd never brought it up and, in hindsight, I'm grateful. The last thing I wanted was to lose his friendship, and he made sure there wasn't any lingering weirdness between us. We carried on like normal—him with his teasing and me with volleying smart retorts in his face—and nothing between us changed.

Sure, Patrick can act like a troll sometimes, and maybe he jokes around too much for some people's liking, but I appreciate his humor. It's how we first became friends.

I know, maybe we seem like an unlikely pairing, but during our very first Eagle Gate assembly, Lulu—*not* Bon Bon—and I sat together. We'd been close friends in middle school, so it was nice to have familiar company. I remember looking around and thinking half the girls looked like they were already in college, but Lulu reminded me that they were seniors, and we'd look like that, too, when we were older.

I thought about that, and I couldn't picture it—this seemed light-years away—and as I was trying to imagine myself taller with glossier hair, a crumpled ball of paper hit me square in the forehead.

A few seats over, a brunet boy with a cropped haircut snickered. This was Patrick, of course.

"*Read it*," he whisper-hissed as the guy next to him elbowed him and said, "Hey!"

Lulu rolled her eyes. "Don't read it."

But I'd snatched the paper from the floor and uncrumpled it because I was curious. In heavy black ink it said *Do you want to be my girlfriend?*

My face flamed, my skin growing warmer by the second. I didn't even know this guy and he was asking *me* out? It didn't make any sense. Maybe he thought I was cute? Nobody had ever thought I was cute before, so for someone to single me out made me feel kinda special.

"No, that's not for you," the guy next to him said. "Pass it down!"

Oh. Right. Why would I assume it was for me? So I did

what he asked, which made Patrick the Instigator laugh harder. So glad he found my humiliation hilarious.

He made sure to *really* let the joke sink in when he found me after school that day. Lulu had ditched me for the artsy crowd. They were all gathered in a huddle near the exit, and I was too intimidated to introduce myself, so I started down the sidewalk without her, accepting I'd have to walk home alone.

"Hey, you!"

I turned to see Assembly Boy striding confidently onto the sidewalk behind me, a wicked grin on his face.

"Watch out for stalker boys asking you out on your way home!" he hollered, laughing.

For the second time that day, my face flushed. But I wasn't about to let him have the last word, so I placed my hands on my hips and yelled, "You mean, *you*? You freak."

This only made him laugh harder. What a weirdo. What was his deal, anyway? Did I have a sign on my back that said *Make me the butt of your joke, please! I'm begging!*

"Hey," I went on. "What's your name, anyway?"

He cupped his ear. "*What?*"

He hadn't bother to come closer, so I wrapped my hands around my mouth and shouted, "You have a *name*? Or should I call you Gigglebox?"

"Oh, it's Patrick!" he offered, waving.

I wasn't amused.

"Well, shut up, *Patrick*!" I tossed back, then whirled on my heel and headed home. I heard him laughing as I rounded the corner.

But then he started sitting across from me at lunch. He

wouldn't even say hi—just plop his lunch tray down and start rambling about science homework or the weather or the best place to eat hot pot like we'd already been in the middle of a conversation. That's how I discovered he liked karaoke and soccer and stand-up comedy. I also learned he had a younger sister named Pearl, who went to the middle school that was my former school's biggest rival. Patrick had gone there, too, which is why I hadn't met him before.

After a few weeks, my guard lowered. Our friendship blossomed. I started looking forward to him joining me for lunch and for our walk home after school. Since he lived two streets down from me, we began making the journey together. One of us would always wait for the other to emerge from the building, and then we'd set off.

Soon enough, we were inseparable. I helped him with his English essays, tweaking his vocabulary and syntax, and he helped walk me through balancing chemical equations. We did everything together—school projects and marathoning our favorite shows and wandering around town when we were bored. Maybe I'd started liking him as more than a friend because we'd grown so close over the years. I'd been pretty heartbroken when he'd turned me down, but at least that hadn't affected our friendship.

"Well, good," Dad says, wiping his moustache with his napkin. "Don't need boys distracting you this year."

I shovel the rest of my toast into my mouth to avoid answering. Note to self: Do not bring up New Boy Joe around Dad. Ever.

"Okay." I spring to my feet. "I'm leaving for school."

"Tell Bon Bon I say hi."

I clear my plate at the sink and turn back to the table. "Oh my god, Dad. You're ridiculous."

I grab my bag and head for the door, swinging it open just as Subwayboy emerges from his apartment. I gasp and slam the door so fast you'd think I was preventing a swarm of hornets from invading our home.

Dad swivels around. "Forget something?"

"Um—no, I—" I panic. "I forgot to tell you to have a good day!"

"Oh, okay." He levels his gaze. "Have a good day. Don't forget to focus in calculus."

"Yep." I wonder if enough time has passed. Is he still out there? "Absolutely."

I don't move.

Dad raises his brows. "Are you sure everything's—?"

Faintly, I hear the elevator doors close.

My hand flies to the doorknob. "Everything's dandy!" I chirp, even though this is the furthest thing from the truth. Oh no, is this going to become my new routine? Waiting until the coast is clear? "Just super! Love you. Bye!"

TWELVE

SARA

"'The seemingly interminable war was won,'" I read, eyes trained on my paper. "'The prodigiously prolonged battle had finally permanently ended. At last, what they'd waited for all along, from the very beginning, had taken place. But all of this monumental effort, at what cost?'"

The class bursts into applause. I blush. I'd put a ton of effort into my history essay, making sure I accurately answered the prompt while sprucing up my sentences with a little flair.

Joe locks eyes with me, clapping louder than everyone else. My stomach flips. Most people only pretend to pay attention during presentations, but it seems like he actually listened. Did I impress him? Gah, I hope I did.

"Nice vocabulary, Sara," Mr. Day says.

I'll take the compliment.

As I sink back into my seat, Joe turns around and gives me a thumbs-up, grinning. My heart flutters. When I glance back to see if Patrick noticed, I find him glowering at the back of Joe's head, shoulders slumped.

Uh, okay. What's his deal?

"Mr. Day?" Rose stands, clasping her hands. "I have an announcement."

Mr. Day checks the clock that hangs over the door. "We've only got five minutes left. The rest of you will read your essays next class." He nods. "Go ahead, Rose."

Rose takes two long steps to the front of the room, then turns to face us. She flips her hair over her shoulder and grins like she's in a Crest commercial.

"Hi, everyone! As you may know, I'm the president of the Newspaper Club," she begins. "Because the school festival is happening next week, Mari and I"—she gestures to her best friend—"are looking for new members to join so we can document all the student experiences happening this year. We hope that by writing about all our organizations and activities, it'll encourage more student participation!"

Eagle Gate's official student festival happens at the beginning of each school year, and it's pretty fun. Student-led organizations set up booths in the courtyard and chat with people who might be interested in joining a new club, activity, or sport. If you want to join, there are sign-up sheets available.

I'd joined Tarot Club with Lulu freshman year before realizing it was more her thing, and I've always been interested in Poetry Club, but I'm too scared to put myself out there. Showing others my writing—my *feelings*? Reading words evoked straight from my heart? Sounds terrifying. I'd rather skydive. Instead, I stick to my blog and notebooks. That's my safe space.

The festival isn't all about clubs, though. There's a dunking booth to raise money for senior prom—students *love* seeing their favorite teacher get drenched—and a life-size chessboard you can play, hosted by Chess Club. The Bake Club will offer sweet treats while a local restaurant caters light bites. Plus, the school usually finds a band to perform live music. Everyone goes and, if they're lucky, finds a community where they feel like they belong.

"Who even reads the newspaper these days?" Patrick mumbles.

Rose shoots daggers at him, frowning.

"I used it the other day," another student jeers, "for *toilet paper*!"

Uproarious laughter booms. Rose crosses her arms, as though waiting for this to die down. She's fearless, I swear. If I were her, I'd want to melt into my seat until the bell rang.

"You guys are idiots," Rose snaps. "And, Patrick, you don't know what you're talking about. People rely on us for the school news."

"Who? Your *mom*?" Patrick says, louder this time.

Ugh, Patrick. Not a good move.

"That's it." Rose is fuming now. "Patrick, you're banned from joining."

"Oh no, *please*. Say it isn't so," he deadpans.

"Okay, class," Mr. Day intervenes. "Let's allow Rose to finish."

"Thank you." She straightens, hands smoothing her uniform skirt. The corners of her glossy lips perk into a smile. "Anyone aside from Patrick interested in joining?"

Silence. And then—

"I'll join."

Joe's hand is in the air.

I immediately sit up straighter. Joe's interested in newspaper? Does this mean he likes writing too? Maybe he does. He appreciated my essay, after all. We could have that in common.

From behind me, Patrick sighs.

"Great! Thanks, Joe." Rose looks pleased with herself. She scans the rest of the room. "Anyone else?"

My heart accelerates like I've been given fresh batteries. I've been too afraid to make a huge change this year, but I can't stay stagnant. I'll never get my first kiss if I don't put myself out there. Joe seems kind. If I joined newspaper, I could get to know him better. And Mr. Day *just* complimented my vocabulary, didn't he?

Maybe this is a sign. My chance to try something new.

Besides, I love my blog. Newspaper involves writing a ton, so it's a seamless transition. And! It'll look excellent on my college applications, which will make Dad proud. It's the perfect idea.

Is this my moment? It is, I decide. I must seize this opportunity!

I raise my hand, suddenly nervous. Oh geez, what am I *doing*?

"Okay so that's Joe and"—Rose's eyes land on me, then bounce away—"every single girl in the class."

Wait, what?

I whirl around. Sure enough, we all have our hands raised high in the air.

How *embarrassing*. I lower mine, hoping Joe didn't notice my acute eagerness. There's a chance he didn't since I'm right behind him, so that's a relief. So much for putting myself out there.

"We can't have every girl in class," Rose continues. "That's too many contributors."

There's a chorus of groans. Someone else says, "That's not fair."

Joe raises his hand again. All eyes zero on him. Including mine. I get a little daydreamy as I focus on him. Everyone at Eagle Gate wears the same uniform blazer, but he somehow pulls it off better than anyone.

"May I make a suggestion?" He clears his throat. "Maybe everyone could apply by submitting a sample essay. I think that could narrow it down."

"*Fantastic* idea." Rose beams. "Thank you, Joe."

An essay. It makes sense—but Rose is president. That means she's in charge of reading these essays. What if I work really hard on mine, pouring time and effort into every single sentence until it's polished to perfection, and then she thinks it's trash? Worse than trash: seeping street sewage. Would she make fun of me? Maybe even read it to the entire class? *Everyone, listen to this silly little essay Sara Lin submitted! It's so tragic!*

No, thank you. Newspaper Club isn't worth all that humiliation.

I'll just have to find another way to put myself out there this year.

THIRTEEN

PATRICK

Look, I don't want to sound jealous or anything, but what's so great about Joe, anyway? He reads the newspaper and takes it seriously? *Oooh*, what an academic. A scholar! Let's award him a Pulitzer.

Man, gimme a break.

Newspaper Club is so old-school, though I guess retro's coming back around. Whatever. All I'm saying is I expected better from Sara.

I'm by her side the second we step into the hall after class. "So, you're joining that stupid club, then?"

Her hands clench around her shoulder strap. "Are you kidding? No way."

We wander down the hall. Students coming from the other direction maneuver around us.

"Why?" I press. She raised her hand in class for a reason. I'm not that dense. "Isn't this your chance to get closer to Joe?

I thought that was your new goal in life. It's all you've been talking about lately. I read your blog, remember?"

She glances around—probably to make sure Joe didn't overhear—before narrowing her eyes. "You read my blog," she repeats.

I fold my arms across my chest. "Duh, Sara. I've been reading it for ages."

"Okay, then." She stops walking, attempting to size me up like she's not several inches shorter than me. "You could've said I should join because I'm a good writer."

Even though she's trying to hide it, there's hurt behind her eyes. Hold on. Did I get it wrong? I never thought Sara would take writing seriously. She insists her blog is for fun, something just for her. She even made me pinkie swear I wouldn't tell anyone about it. Privileged best friend information. I'd never betray that.

But I watched her face light up when she read her history essay—and when she got that huge round of applause when she finished. She's always loved writing assignments. I'm pretty sure it's the only type of homework she enjoys. Maybe she feels like she can only put her writing out there if it's for schoolwork. And if that's the case, it makes sense why she'd want to join Newspaper Club.

"Oh, uh," I backtrack. "That too. You *are* a good writer, Sara. A great one, even."

A satisfied glow washes over her features. Then she grins, turns on her heel, and heads in the opposite direction.

"Nah," she says over her shoulder. "Not my kind of thing, anyway."

I sigh. Sometimes I think the only way to get Sara out of her self-conscious bubble is to nark and needle her until I get a reaction. After all, the kiss bet worked. She went up to a total stranger and asked to kiss him! Never in a million years did I think she'd do that.

And because I read her blog, I know she's desperate for a change this year. She's Shy, Timid, Second-Guessing Sara. She's had a million crushes—including one on me last year—but no boyfriends. And I know she's a romantic. If I don't get involved, I'm afraid she'll *never* put herself out there.

So that's why I say, loud enough to ensure she can hear, "*Chicken.*"

She pauses, twisting around to glare right at me before continuing on her way.

Sara's not really angry, of course. This is how we operate. I provoke and taunt and tease; she tries to prove me wrong. And I think she will. If Newspaper Club is the outlet that will get her writing in front of people, then I hope she considers trying.

FOURTEEN
SARA

Stupid Patrick. How dare he call me a chicken?

Well, I *did* backslide into a lie. I love writing. Patrick knows this. There's a good chance I'd love writing for the school newspaper—except when I said it wasn't my kind of thing.

This is so typical of me. I'll work myself up until I have enough courage, and then completely wuss out. My tutoring session with Subwayboy yesterday is a prime example.

I'm afraid of what people will think, and it's my fear that holds me back. How do people walk around with so much confidence? It's baffling. Everyone's probably clued in on some big secret to living effortlessly. Meanwhile, I'm over here trying not to make a fool of myself.

But I'm never going to romanticize my life if I don't summon enough courage to *try*.

"Yeah, Joe! You can sign up right here."

Up ahead, Rose and Joe are gathered near the student

bulletin board. I slow my pace, pretending to fix my shoulder strap when, really, I'm eavesdropping.

Joe takes the pen from her hand then scribbles his information on the sign-up sheet. "You sure I don't need to apply first?"

"No, no. It's fine!" Rose tosses her gleaming hair and leans closer to him. "You can even be in charge of applications."

"Uh, you really think that's okay?"

"Of course." She releases this tinkling laugh. Even I can tell it's over-the-top. "You're so silly."

Joe returns her pen, then says something I can't make out because now their backs are to me. They're already walking away.

Once they're gone, I approach the bulletin board. Since the school year just started, sign-up sheets clutter every square inch of free space. My eyes roam over the options. MOVIE CLUB! CHEER TRYOUTS! ANIME CLUB! And then—there it is—NEWSPAPER CLUB!

Joe's name is written in neat capital letters. His phone number is on the line next to it. I press my lips together. I guess I really am a chicken, because I wouldn't dare cross Rose's path. It's clear she's interested in him—giggling and giving him preferential treatment. If this was a movie, she'd play the pretty, popular blond who gets the attractive new guy. There's no way I can compete with her, so why bother?

I check the time on my phone. Tutoring starts in ten minutes, which means I have time to pop into the bathroom and collect myself before dealing with the Subwayboy problem.

It's quiet in here. Good. I need to think. Except I wind up fiddling with my hair, trying mimic Rose as I toss my short bob. It doesn't work. My hair sort of flies upward before landing out of place. No wonder I'm practically invisible.

Maybe I can channel her confidence if I practice.

I pull out my phone and pretend to dial Joe's number. "*Oh*, why hello there. Is this Joseph?" I attempt to flutter my lashes but instead of giving *cute*, it looks like I'm malfunctioning. So I stop. "It's me, Sara Lin. *Yeah*. I'm calling to let you know I'm joining Newspaper Club. I heard you're doing auditions? Wait—it's not auditions. What is it?"

"*Psst.*"

My heart attempts to jailbreak from my chest. "Agh! Who's there?"

Lulu glides out of the last stall. I didn't even know she was in here.

"Oh god, Lulu. You scared me."

"I sense your distress, Sara. It's about a boy." Lulu slithers toward me. "Do you want me to read your fortune? I can help you get your man."

I consider this. Lulu's been into astrology for as long as I've known her. She's a Leo—she's told me a gazillion times—and knows all about moon phases and retrograde and, most recently, tarot. Sometimes I'll look over at her table at lunch and find her shuffling her deck and reading someone's cards.

It can't hurt, can it? It's not like I'm killing it on my own. May as well see what my fortune has in store. And at this point, I need all the help I can get.

She must sense I'm about to give in because she grabs my hand and tugs me toward the last stall. There's a sign on the door that says OUT OF ORDER, but this doesn't stop her.

Once we're inside, I realize she's transformed the space.

She's thrown a blanket over a stack of books to make a table, and two velvet floor cushions sit on either side. Twinkling string lights drape over the stall's wall, creating a moody atmosphere.

But—uh. Where the heck is the toilet? I'm scared to ask.

Lulu's silver-contact-lensed eyes greet mine as she lowers herself onto a cushion. "You shouldn't be afraid of joining Newspaper Club, Sara."

Ever since she began hanging out with the artsy kids, Lulu does her makeup in this cool, bold way. Deep mauve eyeliner with shimmery dark eyeshadow. Her staple gold hoops dangle from her ears, matching the eccentric gold jewelry she's collected on her fingers. She told me once her grandmother gave them to her, along with the knitted cap she's wearing, a ribbon threaded through and tied neatly in the back.

I admire Lulu for having her own unique style. It's hard to accomplish when you go to a school requiring uniforms.

I kneel on the cushion opposite her. "Uh, wait—how do you know I—?"

"There's someone new who's started showing interest in you." She shuffles her cards. "Beware. This might cause trouble."

What? *Trouble?* That's the last thing I need. I'm already on thin ice with Dad and calculus, and he's the one who told me to stay very far away from boy problems.

But my curiosity gets the best of me.

"Who?" I urge. "Is it Joe?"

She shrugs. Three cards fall from the deck, landing face down. "Or! This *could* mean it'll be awesome."

I crook a brow. So mysteriously vague. Which one is it?

Lulu flips the first card over. "This one says *stay away from the new kid. He's no good for you.*"

I lean over the table, inspecting. There's a smiling gray moon on this card. How cute. That seems harmless enough, but wait—

"Where does it say that?" I scratch my head. "And which new kid? Is it Joe? Or Subwayboy—he's also new."

Instead of answering, she reveals the second card. "Ah, just as I thought."

Thought *what*?

"What's it say?" The eagerness in my voice is apparent. "Is it about Joe? Or Subwayboy? Or Patrick—?"

Lulu dips her head low, as if bowing to the cards, and closes her eyes. She stays like this for several seconds. Then, ever so slowly, she lifts her head. Her silver eyes bore into mine, and I stare back, waiting. If she's going for suspense, it's working. My fingertips tap the table nervously.

"It says," she says breathily, "you're gonna *die*."

I reel back. "What! Lulu, come on."

"Oh, no, sorry." She squints at the card, nose hovering inches from it. Then her head jerks upright. "I always mess this one up."

She falls quiet, full concentration mode activated. I inch closer, antsy, wondering if there's something about this card that I can interpret myself. The image looks kind of like a court jester, and just as I'm racking my brain to figure out what it could mean, she slams her palms on the table, scaring the *bejeezus* out of me.

"A-ha!" She snaps her fingers. "It says *someone will try to steal your man*!"

My nose crinkles. What on earth? That can't be right.

"Who?" If it's true, then I need context. "Can you be more specific?"

Lulu moves her hands over the cards as though she's fanning a flame. "Go in peace, child. Your fortune has been read."

"Wait, Lulu—"

"May the wind in the east combine with the one in the west." She slaps her hands together over her head, closing her eyes. "And may you have better outcomes than your terrible fortune!"

"Hold on—"

Before I know what's happening, she stands, then kicks open the door. It hits the wall with a loud *thud.*

"Now get out of my stall." She grins. "Or you'll be late for tutoring."

What choice do I have? I rise from my place on her cushion and make my grand exit.

Whatever. I don't believe in this hocus pocus, anyway. What does she even know? Someone stealing my man? Ha! This requires me to *have* said man, like that would ever happen.

Thanks for nothing, Bon Bon.

Shaking my head, I thrust open the bathroom door and make a sharp right turn, but because I'm not paying attention to my surroundings, I smack directly into someone's torso.

Ow.

I'm stepping back when a voice says, "Oh geez! Sorry about that!"

And as I glance up, I realize who I've mistakenly bumped into—and that person is none other than Joe.

FIFTEEN

SARA

"Oh my gosh," I blurt, flustered. "I'm sorry!"

I just walked smack-dab into Joe. *Joe!* Ah! What are the odds?

Genuine concerns splays over his face. "Are you okay?"

What a gentleman, asking if I'm okay when *I'm* the one who collided with *him*!

"I—um." What are words? Say something, Sara! "I'm good!"

Joe gives me this shy smile, and *oh*. It's really cute. "Okay. Good."

"Good," I repeat, as though this is the one and only word I possess in my personal lexicon. My mouth opens again and . . . I'm suddenly rendered speechless. I couldn't string a sentence together if my life depended on it. Nouns? Verbs? What are those?

And now we're just staring at each other as this awkward pause stretches on. My face grows more scarlet by the second.

Soon I will transform into the same color as a fire truck, setting a Guinness World Record for Deepest Shade of Red a Human Can Turn.

He tugs a hand through his hair. This is so awkward. *I'm* so awkward! What am I even doing?

"Um, okay." It comes out more like a squeak. "Bye!"

And then I sprint down the corridor, curve around a corner, and flatten my back against the wall.

Ugh. Why did I do that? I could have asked him about Newspaper Club! Or what school he attended before transferring. Literally said anything else besides *good.* Good?! How many times did I even say that? What is wrong with me?

It's official. When it comes to boys, I'm doomed.

Sighing, I keep walking until I've entered the library. Patrick's sitting at the study table Subwayboy and I occupied last week, but Oliver's nowhere in sight. That's good, considering I'm early on purpose.

I slump into the seat next to Patrick and tug my disguise from my shoulder bag, popping my glasses on my face.

Patrick sets his phone down, observing me. "How long are you going to pretend you're not the creepy girl from the subway?" As I'm pinning my bangs back, he adds, "Not that I care, or whatever."

"Listen, I'll tell him eventually—okay? Just, uh, not today." I twist my scarf around my neck and pull it up to my chin. "Also? I just embarrassed myself in front of Joe ten seconds ago. I can't double embarrass myself right now. I need recovery time, but I'm going to tell him, okay? It's not that easy—"

"Sara." Patrick looks at me like I'm a tiny baby bird who's

just fallen from a nest. "Calm down. You don't have to tell him if you don't want to."

My fingers find my compact at the bottom of my bag. I admire my disguise. "Should I draw a unibrow?"

"Yeah, sure," he deadpans. "While you're at it, draw a fake moustache. That *definitely* won't be weird."

I snap the compact shut. "Fine. I get it." Sighing, I hide my face in my palms, then glance at Patrick between my fingers. He's already back to tapping on his phone. "I *will* tell him, you know. And then? I'll apologize."

"Mm-hmm," he drones. "Sure."

It's clear he doesn't believe me, and why should he? I barely believe myself.

"It'll be incredibly awkward," I go on. "But it's the right thing to do."

"Right, okay." He keeps typing. "Good luck."

This gets on my last nerve. I leap from my seat and slap my hands on the table. My dramatic display gets his attention.

"Why are you being like this? I *am* gonna tell him."

"I'm not sure why you're making this a big deal, but I'm in." He sets his phone down, a mischievous glint in his eye. "Let's turn it into another bet. You tell him *today*."

My hand extends in front of me before I can process what I'm doing. "Deal."

Deal?! Did I really just say that?

Too late. Patrick shakes, and it's done. I've just made another bet.

The door creaks open. I glance over my shoulder to find Oliver shuffling toward us, textbook tucked under his arm, wearing his signature no-nonsense expression of eyebrows drawn together, scowling. It's hard to believe anything in life brings him real joy.

Oliver looks from me, to Patrick, then back to me. "Are you ready to start?"

I nod enthusiastically, already sweating at the thought of fessing up.

Patrick's on his feet, smirking at me as he reaches for his backpack. "I was just leaving." As he passes Oliver, he adds, "So nice to meet Sara's tutor. She's a very normal and nice girl, but I'm sure you know that. Not weird at all, in fact." He tosses me a wink. "Bye!"

I suppress the urge to roll my eyes. What an idiot.

If Oliver finds this strange, he doesn't show it. He just sinks into the seat beside me and flips open his calculus textbook.

"Okay, let's start from the last chapter."

There's no way I'm losing Patrick's bet. So what if I acted like a fool in front of Joe? Now's my chance to make up for it. No more secrets, no more awkward disguises. It's better this way. I'll finally be able to concentrate on math instead of stressing about clearing the air.

"Um, Oliver?" I lower my scarf. "Before we start, can I talk to you about something?"

He finally looks over at me, giving me his signature unamused expression. "Don't you have a test next week? Can it wait until after?" He's already turned back to the book. "Let's go over your homework from yesterday, then we'll move on to the next lesson. Convergent and divergent series. Then, if a series converges, we'll determine its value. You'll see—but stop me if you have any questions."

Gah! Subwayboy, you're making this confession very difficult.

I slide over the homework Mr. Day handed back earlier today. It's been graded already, and only half my answers are correct.

Oliver studies it for a minute and then says, "Okay, let's start with this one." He taps the first problem with his pencil. "This process is complicated, so listen carefully."

If he wants to get down to business, fine. Go ahead. Let's study! But at the end of this session—oh, just you wait, Subwayboy. I'm going to tell you everything. Because I, for one, am not chickening out this time. Nope. Not me. Today's the day I become a little braver. Wait and see, Patrick. I'm *not* losing this bet.

As Oliver carries on about series, my brain feels like a marshmallow roasting over an open fire. Unfortunately, unlike said marshmallow, nothing is sticking. I'm barely following Oliver's lesson, unsure what, exactly, I can ask that will make this easier. All the formulas blur together, and my eyes glaze over.

"Hey," Oliver snaps. "Are you listening? Does this series converge or diverge?"

"Uh—"

"First you have to write the partial sums." He demonstrates in his notebook. "So this sequence diverges, which means the series also diverges. Do you see?"

"Um. Yeah."

A lie, but before I can correct myself, he continues on.

"Okay. You do the next one."

I pick up my pencil and freeze. My head pounds. Which formula do I use for this again? There are so many. They're all starting to look the same too.

After a moment, he sighs.

"Remember, this formula," he begins, tapping at the section in his textbook. "It looks like this."

He jots it down on my worksheet, going over the problem, but soon enough I'm lost again. He may as well have said purple potatoes equal X but Y equals turkey legs, and XYZ equals blah, blah, *blah*.

I keep nodding along like it will magically unlock in the math portion of my brain, but it doesn't. Then Oliver moves on to the next lesson, showing me how to find the derivative of functions. But, oh! This requires algebra in order to evaluate the limit, which involves multiple steps in order to get an answer.

By the time we get through one stinking problem, my brain is on fire.

"Well, that's time." Oliver closes his textbook. "Any questions?"

Uh, yeah. Just one. *Why* am I so bad at this?

"No," I mumble, rubbing my temples.

"Right, well, we started your homework, so do the rest for next time and we'll review it together." He starts packing his backpack, not bothering to look at me. "Oh, and what did you want to talk about?"

That's right. The bet. I have to tell him—except I'm not prepared. We did so much math that I haven't had a second to think about what I'd say. How do I even begin? Maybe *So, take the subway often?* No—what about *Anything weird happen to you lately? Like some stranger asking you to kiss her out of nowhere? Funny story . . .*

Ack! I need to workshop this.

"Nothing," I mutter, shifting my gaze to my shoes. "Never mind."

I feel him watching me as I stuff my textbook in my bag and throw the strap over my shoulder. When I gather the courage to peer up at him, he's palming the back of his neck. Almost like he's nervous. No—aggravated? I have no idea. He's more difficult to solve than a freaking derivative function.

Maybe confessing would come easier if he was friendlier. Instead, he's always staring at me like I've sprinkled dirt on his ice cream. It's very off-putting. Someone should let him know. Not me, of course, because I don't currently have a death wish.

He lets out a long sigh, then steps around me and exits without another word. I wait until I'm sure he's gotten a long head start, then unwrap the scarf from around my neck. So much for bravery and courage. Where's my confidence?

Can't I do *anything* right?

SIXTEEN

PATRICK

I'm heading to lunch with Sara the next day when she releases a squeal and ducks behind me.

"What the—?"

"*Shh!*" she hisses.

From a distance, I spot the reason for her distress. Oliver saunters toward us, a sour grimace pasted across his mouth. Is he always in a bad mood or something? What's his deal?

I puff my chest out like it'll help hide Sara—it's a good thing she's so short—and nod politely as he passes. A casual bro nod, if you will. New Kid only cocks an eyebrow, then shoots me a strange look before disappearing into the cafeteria.

What did I do to deserve that? Nothing, that's what. Some people have no manners.

"That's the math tutor I was telling you about," a junior gushes to her friend as they stroll past us. "Helped me get an A on my last test—*and* he's cute."

Sara clucks her tongue, emerging from behind me. "Yeah,

right. He's not *that* good," she mumbles under her breath. "And he's mean."

Poor Sara. She texted me last night to explain how awful tutoring went, then admitted she never followed through with the bet. I didn't think she'd have the guts to confess, but I'd secretly hoped she would. If anything, it would have made her life easier.

"Well," I start, "maybe if you'd talked to him like you said you would—"

She sighs then digs into her skirt pocket. "Fine. Here's your stupid bet money." Three measly bucks land in my palm. "I had to dig under my bed for change. It's all I have."

I slide the cash in my back pocket. "Dang, I feel kinda bad now."

She snorts. "No you don't."

I grin, playfully nudging her shoulder. "You're right."

The cafeteria bustles with energy and conversation as soon as we step inside. It always smells a little like chicken soup and Clorox, a weird combination, but recognizable. Shoes squeak across the linoleum as students wander to their lunch tables. Overlapping chatter echoes through the hall, interspersed with laughter.

Lunch is released by grade, so juniors and seniors eat together first. Sophomores and freshman get second lunch. Since Sara and I are seniors, it means we eat together every day. I'd even go so far to say it's how we became friends. I kept finding her at lunch and pestering her with random conversation, and she eventually chimed in.

I can't explain why I was drawn to her, really, but I knew from the beginning she had a vibe. She's giggly and fun to be around, matching my energy and cracking jokes almost as often as I do. Who wouldn't want to be around someone like that?

We go through the motions of grabbing a hot meal before finding our usual seat. As I'm unfolding my napkin, Sara places her elbow on the table and cups her chin in her hand.

"Just look at him." She sighs wistfully. "How is he so perfect?"

I follow her yearning gaze. Of course. She's looking at Joe.

"I've been thinking," she goes on, "I'd love someone like Joe to be my first kiss."

I nearly choke on a piece of chicken I've just popped in my mouth. "You're such a cliché. Just kiss whoever. What does it even matter?"

It's not like we haven't talked about this stuff before, but it hasn't come up in a while. I used to think of Sara as my second sister back when we first started high school. Sure, I teased her a lot—and I still do—but we can talk to each other about anything.

So when she admitted last year she had feelings for me, I didn't know what to do. If I'd felt the same way, I would've told her. But I didn't. And I'm not the type to lead someone on—that's just cruel. I could never do that to my best friend. Honesty was the best route, but I still hate the way it crushed her.

Anyway, that was forever ago. She's moved on, and why wouldn't she?

I just didn't think she'd move on to Hotshot Joe.

"I'm not gonna *kiss whoever.*" She does a very poor impression of me. "Why do you think I've been saving my first kiss for so long?"

"*Saving?*" I laugh. "Yeah, I'm sure it's been a *real* struggle rejecting all the guys lining up to kiss you." I uncap my water bottle and take a drink. "Besides, it's not that hard to kiss someone."

"Hey, guys."

Tammy grins at us as she slips into a seat beside me.

Sara leans over her tray. "Hey, Tammy."

What does Sara need to save her first kiss for? It's been a minute, but I've kissed a few girls. It's no big deal. She builds things up in her head all the time, and this is one of them. I need to show her it's all very casual.

And that's when I get an idea. A *great* idea, even.

"I'll show you," I tell Sara. "Just watch."

I turn to Tammy, cupping my hands around her face and—wow. Her skin's pretty soft. I don't think I've noticed something like that before. I've also never noticed she's got a cluster of light-brown freckles scattered across her nose. But then her clear blue eyes widen in confusion as I begin pulling her in close, *closer*—

Smack!

My hands fly to my cheek as Tammy grabs her tray and storms off, announcing to the table behind ours that "*Patrick is a big fat pig!*"

Well, that backfired.

"You know you deserved that, right?" Sara spears a piece of chicken with her fork. "And that was definitely sexual harassment. Don't even think about trying that again."

"That hurt." I whirl around and catch Tammy's attention. "I was *joking*."

"Your joke wasn't funny," Tammy lobs back, turning away in a huff.

The girls around her scowl at me, whispers already circulating around the table. My face reddens, and I'm suddenly hot. Did someone crack the heat in here or what?

"Fine." I focus on Sara. "That didn't go as planned, but you get the drift."

"Patrick, I don't want to have my first kiss to just 'get my first kiss over with,'" she explains, her attention jumping from me to Joe. "What's wrong with falling in love with someone first?"

Love? Since when has Sara wanted to fall in *love*? Seems like a gargantuan waste of time. Love means worrying about another person, making sure they're happy and planning dates and always thinking about them. Plus, love is complicated. You have someone else's feelings to consider about, well, *everything*. When would you have time to do anything else?

"You watch too many rom-coms," I say, scooping up some rice. "They set unrealistic expectations."

Sara blushes. "So someone falling in love with me is unrealistic?"

"No, I didn't say that." Geez, I need to explain myself better. I set my fork down. "I'm saying most guys don't think about kissing like that."

"Whatever." She casts her eyes down at her tray and takes another bite. After she swallows, she goes on. "Just because you don't believe in love doesn't mean I'm not going to have my perfect first kiss." Her eyes drift over to Joe again. "I bet Joe is a perfect gentleman. Just look at him. He looks like he cares, you know?"

From across the cafeteria, Joe passes someone a napkin, laughing at a joke we can't hear. He's sitting at Rose's table, along with Mari and a few guys on the track team. Looks like he's made himself right at home.

"You're saying Joe will fall in love with you, then kiss you? Just like that?" I snap my fingers. "Even though you haven't shared *one* conversation with the guy."

"It's not easy when he's that hot, you know." She tucks her hair behind her ear. "But I'm sure with time he'll get to know me and realize how funny, cute, smart, sensitive, beautiful, and gorgeously charming I can be."

There's no denying Sara's all of those things, but she's never put herself out there enough to show anyone but me and Vicky.

"Ha, yeah, right." I snort. "We both know you're too chicken."

She scoffs. "What? No, I'm not."

"Need I remind you of yesterday?" I point out. "You can barely utter a single word when you're around Joe. There's no way you'll engage in a real conversation where he actually gets to know you."

I'm laying it on thick, but Sara needs a challenge. If I'm an instigator, so what? Maybe she'll finally do something about it.

"I can so," she counters, folding her arms over her chest in defense.

"Nope." I pop my *p*, which further infuriates her. Her round amber eyes narrow. "You're too chicken. It's who you are, you know? Accept it. There's nothing wrong with that."

"*Patrick*," she snaps. "I am *not*."

"Are sooooo," I singsong, fully getting under her skin now.

"Shush, you evil dorkasaurus rex."

"*You* shush, bucko."

"*Bucko?* That's the best you got?"

Heads swivel in our direction. Whoops. We're kind of loud. People are starting to stare. Sara, however, doesn't seem to notice.

"Nah, we both know you're a scaredy cat," I press. "Give it up now, Sara Lin."

"Okay, you know what, butthead?" She thrusts a finger at me. "Let's make a bet."

"Bring it on." I rub my hands together like I'm a corrupt villain in a fantasy novel. "How much am I making today?"

"No more money," she huffs. "This time, the loser has to do the other's homework for a week."

"Are you serious? Sara, you don't even do your own homework."

"I will." She sticks out her hand, fearless in this very moment. "Deal?"

Sara hates homework more than she hates losing money, so this may work in my favor. And if she talks to Joe, then she can stop talking to me *about* Joe. I swear, if I have to hear her describe how dreamy his hair is when it falls over his forehead *one* more time—

I shake her hand. "Fine, deal."

A smile reaches her eyes. She looks extremely pleased with herself. But before I can get another word in, she takes her last bite of food, leaps to her feet, and grabs her empty tray.

"Where are you going?" I call after her.

"I have until the end of the day tomorrow," she tosses over her shoulder. "I'm gonna go prepare conversation topics."

That dork. Preparing conversation? Who even does that? Wait, is she going to practice on index cards?

Ha! She so would.

I glance over at Joe. He's listening politely as Rose goes on about something—probably her favorite conditioner or something equally trivial—and then I wonder if this bet was a mistake. I can't tell if Joe seems into Rose, but if he is, then that love story is inevitable. Rose always gets what she wants.

Agh, I should really cool it with the bets.

SEVENTEEN

SARA

"How am I so good at winning these bets?" Patrick folds his arms across his chest, puffing it out in victory. "Seriously, I'll have to find a new hobby this week since you'll be busy finishing all my homework."

A rock sits in the pit of my stomach as I watch Joe walk out the school gates the next day. It's official. I didn't talk to Joe at all. Not even a teeny hello.

I suck. Worse? I'm so disappointed in myself.

Here's the thing. I'd prepared. *Over*prepared, even. I mean, last night I'd stayed up late making flashcards and practicing my opening lines in front of the mirror. I tried on different tones, seeing how fluttery and high my voice could go, until I landed on one somewhere between friendly and approachable.

Then, to ease my anxiety, I'd blogged about how I wouldn't let my fear get the best of me. I could do this! I talked to Patrick every day, didn't I? If I pretended Joe was Patrick, maybe that would make it easier.

I *tried.* Really, I did. In history, I reached out to tap him on the shoulder. My plan was to say I loved his history essay, but then my throat constricted and my hand jerked back into my lap like I'd been shocked. Why? Because I imagined my words coming out all wrong—*I thought your essay on the Fronch Reebolusion was good. I mean Fresh Revolution! Agh! French! Like the country. Um, just wanted to tell you!*—and, ugh, how embarrassing. I'd die.

Nope. History wasn't the time to talk to Joe, I decided.

But I wasn't worried, because after lunch we had gym class together. *This* was my golden opportunity.

As Joe was stretching out his quads, I inched closer to him. The sun shone down on us and a crisp breeze blew, somehow making his hair look even more perfect. Like one of those runway models walking toward a giant fan. I could feel Patrick watching from afar while he stretched one arm across his chest, and suddenly I was emboldened. *Watch this,* I thought, and then, after clearing my throat, I attempted to speak.

"Uh—d-do you want, um?"

You know the tiny pitter patter sound a mouse makes? Yeah, that was about as loud as my vocal range went. Joe didn't hear me. Instead, his attention turned to Rose, who sashayed over to his other side, eyelashes fluttering.

"Hey, Joe." She spoke loudly and clearly. "Want to be my partner?"

Joe beamed, turning his back to me. "Sure."

They walked to an open space near Coach Garcia, and I was left standing there like a total dork rocket. When I glanced over at Patrick, he was cackling into his hands.

My final opportunity was calculus. I'd worked up the courage to say, *Hey, did you understand yesterday's homework?* Easy enough, right? But every time I opened my mouth, it was like an octopus had wrapped its tentacles around my throat. The bell rang, and Joe slid from his seat and moved out the door before I could even think about catching up.

Which brings us here. Now.

Patrick tugs me into a headlock and ruffles my hair. I elbow him in the stomach, which causes him to immediately release me as he doubles over. I don't even feel bad.

As I'm storming away, he bellows, "No need to be a sore loser."

Ignoring this, I storm inside. I'm so not in the mood for his schtick. As if today wasn't already the worst, it's not even over. Because I have stupid tutoring.

I hang my head as I wander to the library, pausing just outside the door. Why do I always take Patrick's bait? Now I'm stuck doing his homework too—and Oliver's probably going to assign me extra tutoring homework. I'm so mad. Maybe it's unfair to take this out on Patrick, but he's the reason I'm in this mess in the first place, including the ongoing mess with Subwayboy.

A lick of fire lights up inside me. Maybe I wasn't brave enough to talk to Joe today, but something *must* change.

I'm digging through my shoulder bag, my fingers closing around my glasses, when I pause. Yes, I could put on my disguise again, but today's already proven I'm a major failure. Do I really need to chicken out with this? Shouldn't I take a risk? If I don't, I'm going to have to keep hiding forever. That's not what I want.

Come on, Sara. Do something brave, for once.

Taking a deep breath, I stride into the library as myself—no disguises.

My heartbeat increases with each step I take. When I gather the nerve to look at Oliver, I find him staring at me with his usual *I'm way too cool for this and also I'm so bored* expression. Well, okay, then. That's good? Or maybe not? I have no idea.

I pull out the chair across from him and sit, palms sweating. He's studying me now, eyebrows raised, but his expression is still inscrutable. Does he recognize me? Is he going to call me out as Subwaygirl? Hash everything out—here—in public? What if he stomps out and refuses to tutor me? What on earth will I tell Dad?

But, no. Instead, he says, "What happened to your glasses?"

"Uh"—I grasp for an excuse—"they broke."

He's already flipping through his textbook, unbothered. Like it doesn't matter if I have glasses or not. "Oh. Well, let's start."

Okay? So why ask me in the first place? I swear, rocks are easier to read than this guy.

I heave a dramatic sigh, leaning back. "Fine."

Ugh, I *really* don't want to do this. If there was any justice in this world, a light catastrophe would occur at this very moment. Nothing deadly or life altering, but maybe a rumbling thunderstorm that knocks out the electricity, forcing us to go home for the day.

His eyes leap to mine. "Did you do your homework?"

Okay, what is with this guy? Really? He doesn't even say

hello like a normal, friendly human. No, he just sits there judging me, looking like he's permanently sucking on a lemon. Zero pleasantries. Has he never heard of small talk? Or is he allergic to the concept? Straight to business, as always. Math, math, *math*—that's it. Nothing else. It drives me bonkers. Hasn't anyone taught him kindness goes a long way?

If Joe was my tutor, everything would be perfect. We'd be a scene straight from a rom-com. I'd compliment his hair; he'd compliment my smile. I'd understand calculus in two seconds, then he'd say I was the smartest girl in the entire universe and ask me out for ice cream. And then we'd walk around the park until the sun set, just talking and getting to know each other. Maybe I'd even make him laugh.

But no. My life isn't a movie, and I'm stuck here with Scrooge's great-great-grandnephew, who clearly hates my guts.

I drop my forehead onto the table and circle my arms around my head, groaning. (Because—yes—I forgot to do my homework. Is that really a surprise?)

"Today sucks," I moan, miserable.

Oliver sighs. "Guess that's a no, then."

"Have you ever had an opportunity right in the palm of your hands," I hear myself say, "but because you're an idiot, you just . . . let it go?"

"No," Oliver says, dryer than an unused sponge. "Because I'm not an idiot."

I choose to ignore this, popping my head up. "What is wrong with me? I could've just talked to him today. It would have been so easy! But now I have to do *double* the homework, and—worst of all—it's my fault. *Mine.* I'm the one getting myself into these situations! There's no one else to blame." I drop my head again, speaking straight to the table. "My life sucks."

Oops. Maybe I overshared. Typical me. Whatever; he already thinks I'm weird. It's not like I can do anything to change that now. Though, in hindsight, I should have saved the venting for my blog.

He's quiet. Seconds tick by. The silence widens, only growing more awkward.

And then—

"Are you done?"

I jerk my head up and glare at him. "Why are you so rude? Honestly." Then I push myself into a seated position and fold my arms across my chest. "Are you a robot? All you want to talk about is calculus. I mean, you don't even say *hi*. Just—*derivates! series! sequences!* And, okay, yeah, I know you don't like me. That's very clear. I'm not exactly a fan of you either—"

"Hold *on*." Oliver frowns so deeply that, if it curved any lower, it'd be touching the floor. "You *do* know I'm not getting paid to hang out with you, right? I'm here to help you understand calculus."

Okay, fair point.

"Yeah, but—"

"Which is, might I add, proving to be a very difficult task."

"Maybe it's because you suck as a tutor," I volley a reply. "Ever think about that? Also? You need to severely work on your people skills. Perhaps I could tutor *you* in *that*."

The tips of Oliver's ears turn pink. "You're acting childish."

I throw my arms in the air, at my wit's end. "At least ask me how I'm doing! Or if I'm understanding the material.

Maybe if you were nicer, you'd discover I'm actually some calculus genius."

"That makes zero sense, but fine." He leans in closer, staring directly into my eyes. His eyes are this light mossy-green color, and it transports me back to the subway. How he opened them when I was the one moving in close, and the color caught me temporarily off guard. "How was your day? Care to explain why, exactly, you're so upset right now?"

I don't drop my eye contact. Instead, I cross my arms and press my lips together. Let him see how it feels to sit in a long pause. That'll show him.

"Explain?" I finally say. "Why would I? I don't even know you."

Wrong thing to say. Oliver releases a frustrated breath between his clenched teeth and rises to his feet, packing up his bag.

No! I need him. I mean, I don't *want* to need him, but I'm never going to get a good grade on my homework or my calculus test if he's not here to assist me.

"Wait!" I lightly tug the hem of his hoodie as he's turning toward the door. He freezes in place. "I'm sorry, okay? I'm the worst. I didn't mean any of it. I'm just—I'm angry at someone else, and that's not your fault."

He scowls at me from over his shoulder. I must look pretty pathetic, because a second later, his eyes soften. Sighing, he slings his backpack off and returns to his seat.

"Okay," he says dully.

"Okay!" I chirp, bringing as much enthusiasm as I can muster. I start flipping through my textbook at lightning speed. "Let's do this!"

Suddenly, he slaps a palm on my book, preventing me from turning any more pages. "No."

My jaw drops. "No?"

He's studying me curiously, as if trying to solve a very difficult equation. Oh no—does that mean he finally recognizes me? Is he about to bring up the subway incident? Please, *please* don't bring it up now! Not when I've completely made a fool of myself.

"You're too distracted." I'm shocked at how gentle he sounds. It's new for him. "You've got to understand your priorities. Do you want to pass calculus?"

I nod.

"Okay, then stop playing around and take this seriously." He tugs his backpack straps over his shoulders again, standing. "Go take care of whatever's distracting you, then we'll meet up whenever you're ready to focus. Just text me."

And then, without another word, he leaves.

As I watch him go, an unsettled feeling swims in my chest. I slide my forearms on the table and slump over them, groaning. Take care of what's distracting me? What if *you're* distracting me, Subwayboy?

It's hard to concentrate on equations when I don't even know if he remembers me. And yes, it's my fault for never bringing it up, but I also wasn't wearing my disguise. If he recognized me, wouldn't he have said something? Surely, right? I mean, if I were in his shoes, I'd have at least said something like *Hey, you look sort of familiar. Don't I know you from somewhere?* And maybe, if he had said that, I'd have been brave enough to spill the entire truth. Get it off my chest once and for all.

Ugh, whatever. At least now I get a break from calculus. I guess that's a bonus? Well, not if I fail my next test. That's the opposite of a bonus.

Maybe Oliver has a point.

My brain is all over the place because I'm too stressed out focusing on all these little messes. I proved to myself I could walk in here without a disguise. That showed courage. I *am* strong! I didn't backslide into becoming shy, timid Sara Lin. That's not who I'm trying to be going forward.

I sit up, cracking my knuckles. Determination thrums through me.

It's time to take care of one problem at a time. I *have* to start taking matters into my own hands.

EIGHTEEN

PATRICK

"It's great to have one-on-one time with you since Sara's in tutoring so much," I say as Vicky slides my chicken katsu bowl in front of me. "Now we can talk behind her back, and she'll never know."

Since Sara's occupied with tutoring and Tammy's still irked by the stunt I pulled at lunch yesterday, I took the subway to Kiki's Chicken Kitchen alone once school let out. Kiki's is a local restaurant owned by Vicky's mom (who's also Sara Lin's aunt), and it's beloved by everyone in the community, including me.

The interior's covered with sunshine-yellow branding—yellow walls, yellow take-out bags, yellow napkins—and plenty of seating. Before Sara started tutoring, we'd come over here and split a chicken katsu bowl, hanging out with Vicky when there weren't many customers she had to serve. Vicky doesn't mind the job—especially when Sara and I visit—and when it's slow, her mom lets her do homework in the back.

Vicky arches an eyebrow. "Be serious."

"You know I'm kidding." I grab some chopsticks and dig into the steaming rice. "But, hey, ever since the subway incident I keep telling Sara to do these outrageous bets, and she falls for it *every* time. Like, today? I bet her to talk to Joe—he's her new crush—and she couldn't even do that! So now she has to do my homework for a week."

Vicky produces a rag from the front pocket of her apron and wipes down the table next to mine. "She's got a new crush?"

"Yeah, don't you read her blog?"

But Vicky's already at the next table stacking plates on top of each other then discarding them in the bin near the kitchen before returning to my table.

"I haven't had time," she admits.

"He's this new transfer student," I explain. "All the girls are in love with him."

Vicky adjusts her bandana—yellow, surprise, surprise—then reaches for her dishrag. "Huh."

"Anyway, I'm just trying to help her. She told me she wants her first kiss to be with someone she loves, but how can that happen if she can't even *talk* to a guy?" I snort. "I thought if I pressured her with bets, it'd help."

"Did you want to help, or is this really about the money?"

I shrug, using my chopsticks to grab a piece of crispy chicken. "Money is money."

She spares a fast glance at her manager—who's talking to one of the cooks in the back—before sitting across from me. "So—this new guy."

"What about him?"

"Does he feel like competition for you?" She crosses her arms and her lips twist into a smirk. "If all the girls are *in love with him*, he must be supercute, right? So—what? Are you finally going to get the guts to fight for her?"

I pause halfway through chewing. Vicky grins wider, like she's trapped me.

Fight for her? What is Vicky even *talking* about? Sara and I are best friends. That's it. We moved past her having a crush on me before our friendship crashed and burned.

"I don't need to fight for Sara," I protest, narrowing my eyes.

"Patrick, you talk about her *a lot*."

"So? You're her cousin. She's my best friend." I lower my gaze and focus on balancing another bite between my chopsticks. "What else should we talk about?"

"Sure, but you sought me out during my shift to talk about her, which is cool. I love Sara." She rolls my discarded straw wrapper into a ball and tosses it playfully at my chest. "But, like, why?"

I grab the paper from where it fell into my lap and set it on the table, considering this. I don't have many friends, especially guy friends. I have what my parents call "buddies"—guys I'll say hi to in the halls or occasionally talk about sports with—and "acquaintances"—people I share notes and classes with—but none come close to matching what I have with Sara. Besides, why would I need a ton of friendships when I have her?

But if I had more friends, then maybe I'd be hanging out with them right now instead of talking to Sara's cousin *about* Sara. Not that Vicky isn't my friend. We're cool. But Sara's the only thing we have in common.

"We were used to her crushing on you for the longest time," Vicky goes on. "Then last summer she finally gets over you. I mean, that must have affected you, right? What, is she not giving you enough attention anymore, so you have to come here and talk about her?"

"Sheesh, *relax*." I pretend I'm busy wiping my fingers on my napkin, avoiding the heat of her gaze. Why does she have to dissect this, anyway? "Sara and I are just friends. It's like everyone expects us to be more than that, but it's not gonna happen."

When Sara confessed her feelings to me, it was clear Vicky wanted it to happen. And I get it. Vicky's family. You always want to see your family happy. If someone was mean to Pearl or broke her heart, it wouldn't exactly make my day.

But I was honest with Sara, because I really didn't view her as more than a friend. It's not like I *couldn't* imagine kissing her. I've noticed her lips before, like when she smiles or when she puts on this peach lip gloss that makes them extra shiny. And they seem soft . . .

Okay, so maybe I could imagine kissing her—but what if it was weird? Why take that risk and ruin our friendship?

"Why not?" Vicky pushes. "What's wrong with Sara?"

"Nothing, geez." I roll my eyes. "She's great, but I've never thought about her like that. Besides, dating ruins friendships. And that sucks."

"Hmm," Vicky says, thoughtful. She brushes the palm of her hands over her work slacks, as if wiping away invisible dirt. "Feelings may develop now that you've got real competition."

"Man, why do you have to bring this up while I'm trying to eat?" I put another bite into my mouth, swallow, and then say, "We're clearly not on the same page about her."

"Hey, *you're* the one who brought her up." Vicky stands, already heading to another table across from me. "Not me!"

As she produces a receipt for a family who's done eating, I pull out my phone. Sara hasn't updated her blog, and why would she? She's in tutoring right now.

I guess I miss her. But that's normal, isn't it? We do everything together, and now she's focused on other things. Like Joe. And calculus.

And Subwayboy.

That last one makes me shiver. Geez, what if he'd said yes to kissing her? Would they be dating right now? Would she be obsessed with him instead of Joe? Have I ever pictured Sara Lin with a boyfriend before now? No—so why does the mental image get under my skin?

I blink away those thoughts.

The thing is, I hate making bets she keeps losing, but if that's the only way to keep her close, then maybe it's not a bad idea after all.

NINETEEN

SARA

I can hear Led Zeppelin's "Black Dog" blaring down the hall as soon as I step from the elevator, and I already know who's to blame.

Dad.

The muffled music blasts straight into my eardrums when I open the door, where I find him untangling a wad of thick cords. Ah. He's setting up his amp. Somehow he senses I'm standing in the threshold, because he grins as I drop my shoulder bag onto the floor.

"Hey, honey, check it out." He brandishes an arm toward the side table perched beside the couch. "I fixed my record player!"

"I can tell." I have to raise my voice in order to be heard over Robert Plant's *Oh yeahs*. "Our neighbors are gonna complain if you don't turn that down."

He cups an ear. "What?"

My point, ladies and gentlemen.

"Daadddd," I moan, sauntering closer so he can hear me. "I thought I was free from this music after that thing broke."

"What are you talking about?" He starts shimmying his shoulders and, because he hasn't changed out of his professional work attire, it screams *midlife crisis*. "These are classics. Look, AC/DC"—he shoves an album under my nose—"Queen! Only the best in this household."

Shaking my head, I step toward the fridge and grab a sparkling water. "It's too loud, though," I call over my shoulder. "It disrupts my spirit."

"I miss the good ol' days when I'd rock it out on the guitar with ma' mates," Dad says, putting on this terrible British accent.

I shut the fridge. "What are you talking about? You can't play the guitar."

But when I come back into the living room, I find him with a shiny red Fender strapped across his chest. Even I have to admit it's impressive looking, and I know zilch about guitars.

"I will now." He gives the instrument a strum. Dissonant chords scream through the amp. Oh, geez, we're gonna be evicted if he keeps this up. "Now I can play along to all my favorite tunes. Check it out—I learned the chords to Black Sabbath's 'Iron Man.'"

He strums the strings again, except this time the sound comes out bumpy and jumbled. If he realizes it's out of tune, he doesn't show it. Just grins at me, his glasses slipping down the bridge of his nose. Oh, bless him. I guess even dads need hobbies. I shouldn't burst his excitement bubble.

I walk down the hall. "I'll be in my room."

"Wait! I set this up so we could have a jam sesh together."

"I've got homework," I yell over my shoulder, then step into my room and shut my door—which, by the way, does nothing to muffle the whiny sounds emanating from his guitar.

Joy. At least he's in a good mood, which serves me well, because I'm going to have to tell him tutoring didn't go as planned.

Sighing, I change out of my uniform and tug an oversized lemon-yellow sweater over my head, following this by pulling on my softest jeans before collapsing belly first on my bed. I check my phone. No new messages. Blergh. I was hoping Rose would text me back.

I'd wandered over to the bulletin board after Oliver bailed on me earlier, because I'd been determined to do *something* right. Which is why I grabbed Rose's number from the Newspaper Club sign-up sheet and then texted her to ask if it was too late to submit a sample article.

I wonder if she looked at my text, laughed, and ignored it. She probably doesn't think I'd write a good enough article for her club. Maybe I should have texted Joe's number instead—it was right there on the bulletin board next to Rose's. She *did* put him in charge of applications, after all, and he seems like the type who'd respond to a text.

But no—I can't even summon the courage to talk to him over a screen.

Ugh, do I even have time for Newspaper Club right now? Maybe Subwayboy was right. What *are* my priorities? I should text him and apologize. Say we should meet for tutoring tomorrow. There—math! That's one priority down. And if I do that, then Dad doesn't even need to know how spectacularly bad tutoring was today.

I sit up, grab my phone, and type a message to Oliver.

Sara: Hey, sorry about today. Can we meet after school tomorrow?

My message says Delivered. Okay, that wasn't so hard, was it? In fact, it's simpler than speaking face-to-face. At least I don't have to witness him staring at me like my eyebrows have morphed into caterpillars before his very eyes.

Bzzt, bzzt. Another text.

Oliver: Okay

A mysterious boy of few words. Well, great. At least that's done.

Maybe I shouldn't join Newspaper Club. I need to be responsible with my time. If I keep my grades high, it means I have to focus less on scrambling to catch up, which leaves room for me to focus on other things. Like my first kiss. And Joe, maybe. At the very least, I can continue to work up the courage to get to know him.

That's it! If Rose texts me back—and she probably won't—I'll tell her my excuse. I don't have time.

I press my cheek against my pillow and close my eyes. An urge to vent tickles through me, but I have to stop myself from grabbing my laptop and blogging about my day. Because blogging isn't a priority, is it? But it's a release. I always feel better when I get stuff off my chest and out in the open.

My phone buzzes. Adrenaline shoots up my spine as I pick up my phone, but it's only Patrick.

Patrick: Yo!!

Patrick: Did you finish my homework?

Ugh. I almost forgot about the double homework. For a second, I got excited because I thought Rose was texting me.

Is that a sign I should join Newspaper Club?

Sara: Sure bruh. Just finished

Patrick: I don't believe you

Patrick: Do you even know what it is??

Sara: What is it?

Patrick: O___o

Patrick: 300-word essay for English. Topic: my favorite vacation

Sara: lol you want me to make up a random vacation for you?

Patrick: Ha-ha-ha yeah

Sara: My Favorite Vacation: The Time I Took Pearl to the Barbie Museum

Patrick: Oh god

Sara: Don't act like you hated it!

Patrick: Ha-ha-ha-ha XD

A new notification makes my phone vibrate, the alert appearing at the top of my screen. The message is from a number I don't recognize. I swear, if this is one of my dad's friends trying to get hold of him through me again—

Unknown Number: Hi, I heard you're interested in joining the Newspaper Club

Huh, that's weird. This isn't Rose's number. I'd know, because I saved it to my contacts earlier. But I guess I could see who's messaging me.

Sara: who diz???

Unknown Number: Sorry, this is Joe Yang from school

I bolt upright. My heart accelerates, a rapid *ba-bump, ba-bump* rocking in my chest. No, *surely* I didn't read that correctly. So I peek at the message again, rereading it. Then I reread it once more just to make sure I'm not hallucinating.

There's his name. Joe Yang.

Joe Yang from school is texting *me*, Sara Lin, about Newspaper Club.

What on earth?! What do I *do*?

This is what my brain sounds like: AHHHHHHHH.

Before I can think of a way to solve this problem, another text arrives.

Unknown Number: Sorry, Rose gave me your number since I'm in charge of applications

Joe Yang has my number because Rose gave it to him! I could run twenty laps around the park right now. Pure elation zips up my spine as I add his name into my contacts, then position my thumbs to reply.

Sara: Oh, hey! No worries!

Sara: Wazap?

I cringe. Wazap? Why the heck did I write that? Why the heck did I *send* that?

Joe: Just letting you know you can submit your entry to me

Ack, why have I forgotten how to text like a regular, functioning human? What do I write back? Should I send something short, like *okay*—or is that too cold?

Wait. I've got it.

Sara: Okay

Sara: :)

There, a smiley. That's pleasant.

Joe: Can't wait to read it!

Joe: Loved your history paper ;)

I gasp. A winky face? From Joe? Joe who loved my paper?!

I might have a heart attack. Actually, I may faint like I'm a woman in a Victorian drama. Because I've just had my first conversation with Joe Yang. Sure, it's over text, but it still counts.

No more excuses. I'm going to write that essay for Newspaper Club, and it's going to be incredible. Better than anything I've written on my blog, that's for sure. These words will *sing*. They will *move* people. They will *change lives*!

But—oh. What do I write about?

From the living room, Dad strums another chord, the wailing permeating through my door. I laugh. What a goofball. I shouldn't have been so hard on him earlier. He's trying something new, just like me.

Maybe if I rock out with him for a bit, an article topic will pop into my brain. Besides, I could use a break before starting homework.

I'm about to toss my phone onto my bed when it buzzes again, but the notification tells me it's only Patrick. Whatever he wants, it can wait. I need to fill my soul with yacht rock in order to become inspired.

I've got an award-winning article to write, after all.

TWENTY
SARA

"—and listen to your teacher!" Dad's saying as I'm leaving for school the next morning.

"I always do. I'm a perfect angel," I call over my shoulder.

When I joined him in the living room yesterday, he taught me a few chords to Queen's "Crazy Little Thing Called Love." Once I got the hang of it, he swayed his hips and waved his hands high in the air as if pretending he was front row at a concert. He's happiest when he's listening to his favorite music and, as corny as he may be, I love that he's *my* dad.

We never get the chance to bond anymore, not with his hectic work schedule and my after-school tutoring sessions, so I enjoyed his impromptu lesson.

Now that I'm older, he gets stumped on how to connect with me. It's not like he can propose a zoo day or schedule a playdate—I'm not six. But I appreciate that he tries. Even when I'm in a bad mood, I know he makes a conscious effort to hang out with me, all because he cares. Once he googled a plethora of K-pop stars and brought them up at dinner, asking me my opinions on each person. It was really funny, and I ended up educating him for an entire hour.

After we jammed together last night, I went back to my room inspired. That was when I decided to write an article about the local music events happening at our community center. I found a list of concerts online and researched all the artists involved, then I pulled together an entertaining article, making sure all my sentences were clear, concise, and polished—though I did add my own Sara Lin flair. That's important, I've learned. Having a point of view in your writing and using creativity to make it your own. You have to get the message across—the who, what, when, where, why—but you also don't want to sound like a total snoozefest.

Anyway, I think I succeeded.

"Sara Lin?"

I yank my key from the lock and swivel around. There, right before my very eyes, is none other than Joe Yang.

My throat shrinks, its pathway as narrow as a straw. "*Joe?*"

I can't help but gape as I look up at him. What is he doing here? How does he even know where I live? Oh my gosh—did he text Rose to find out? Maybe he came all this way to walk me to school. I try not to audibly swoon at this thought.

He grins that brilliant megawatt smile. "I can't believe you live across from me."

Uh—what? Across from him? Or does he mean diagonally across from him in the other apartments on the opposite side of my hall?

As I try to slot these puzzle pieces together, he just stares at me. Right. This is a conversation. I have to say *something.*

"Uh, yeah." I release an awkward laugh. "So, uh—strange!"

"Hey, you wanna walk to school together?" He adjusts his backpack straps. "I'm just waiting for my little brother. He'll be out in a sec."

Aw, that's so cute. I wonder if he goes to the elementary school a few blocks over, the one I went to before attending Eagle Gate. Of course Joe would walk him there—because he's kind and noble and generous.

"You have a brother?" I say, then resist the urge to slap a palm to my forehead. He *just* said that.

Joe doesn't seem to notice. "Yeah, his name's Oliver."

It's suddenly thirty degrees hotter in the hallway. My face flares, skin reddening. Perspiration gathers on the back of my neck.

No, no, NO! How could this happen? Joe lives with Oliver. Oliver, his brother.

Subwayboy Oliver.

I spin on my heel and face my door so he can't see me panicking. "Um, I forgot—something! I should—"

Too late. The door behind me creaks open.

"There he is," Joe says cheerfully.

I turn around, the scene playing out in slow motion. Subwayboy pushes a sweep of golden hair away from his face, his eyes landing on mine as he pulls the door closed. Then, as understanding sinks in, his expression softens in surprise.

Joe loops an arm around his shoulders, tugging him in close.

"Sara, this is my younger brother, Oliver." He introduces us. "Oliver, Sara goes to our school too. What a coincidence, right?"

They're almost the same height, but they couldn't appear more different. Joe's flop of dark hair is like night to Oliver's lighter strands. Joe's bright smile, full sunshine compared to Oliver's darkening grimace.

I've never seen Oliver look this caught off guard, but a second later, his walls are back up. He looks miffed as he takes Joe's hand and tosses it from around him, stepping to the side and bolting to the elevator.

Well. Okay.

"Don't mind him, he gets like that sometimes," Joe tells me. "You ready?"

"Uh." I swallow. What else am I going to do? "Sure."

The elevator doors open right as we catch up to Oliver. The three of us step inside, and Joe reaches out to press the Lobby button. Oliver tightens his grip on his backpack straps while Joe stares happily at the elevator doors.

I can't believe it. Joe lives right across the hall? This doesn't happen in real life. Not to me, anyway. No, this is something straight from a rom-com.

But that's what I wanted, right? A change! A way to romanticize my life! I'd tried to do this last night when I wrote my article. I pictured myself as a young Carrie Bradshaw, gazing out the window and pouring my heart and soul into this piece. And now this! A love interest right across the way, us bumping into each other this morning. Not only that, but I held an *entire conversation* with Joe. All by myself!

Eeep! Wait until I tell Patrick. He's never going to believe me. Good thing I have those texts with Joe from last night as proof.

So what if he has a sourpuss brother who hates my guts? That's irrelevant. What really matters is allowing this to work in my favor.

Oliver shifts, glaring down at me. How the heck are they even related? And why didn't he inherit an eighth of the people skills Joe has? If he was friendly like his brother, maybe we'd get on better.

"Isn't it wild I was texting you last night about Newspaper Club, and now we find out that we're neighbors?" Joe beams at me. "The world is such a small place!"

I grin, because it's easy to be in a good mood around him. He's so positive.

"It really is."

"I joined Newspaper Club at my old school," he continues. "I was a features reporter."

"Really? That's so cool. Oh—" I reach inside my bag and retrieve my article. "Speaking of, I have my application piece for you."

"Awesome." Joe takes it from me and scans the headline. "Wow, looks great. I honestly can't wait to read it."

I flush. He's easy to talk to. Why was I scared?

"I've been trying to convince Oliver to join." Joe elbows him as we lurch downward. This elevator is ancient, which means it's slower than my grandmother driving through a school zone. "Right, Oliver? But he keeps saying he's too busy tutoring after school. I'm going to keep trying, though, because I think he's a pretty good writer."

Oliver only pops in his earbuds. "I can't hear you."

Joe chucks a thumb at him. "He can totally hear me. He's just too humble to admit he excels at writing."

Of course. I mean, is there anything Oliver *isn't* good at? Aside from all human interactions? Maybe Joe could give him smile lessons in his downtime.

The elevator doors ding open. Oliver darts out like someone's dropped the gnarliest stink bomb.

"He's adjusting," Joe says as we're exiting our building. Oliver's made a conscious effort to stay at least twenty feet ahead of us. "It's been hard for him. I'm a pretty social guy, but he's an introvert. Always listening to music—actually, do you play guitar? I thought I heard Queen coming from your place last night."

Another embarrassed flush takes over my cheeks, but Joe doesn't seem annoyed. Whew. As it turns out, he's curious. So that's how I end up telling him about my dad, and how he fixed his record player and bought a guitar, and how all that inspired me to write my article.

Joe's eyes light up as he listens, nodding enthusiastically and interjecting with things like "Queen is the best," and "What kind of guitar?" And then he tells me they also live with their dad—Mr. Yang, I had no idea he had kids!—although they'd lived with their mom before this, and how she's been getting serious with a guy Oliver hates. Joe doesn't hate anyone, which is easy to believe, but he says this guy isn't exactly friendly. He also tells me about his sister, Meg, who ended up staying with their mom because it would have been awkward if they all left together.

I'm enraptured by these details, so immersed in his life I don't even realize we're approaching the school's double doors. My eyes must have transformed into two gigantic hearts that were trained on Joe this entire time, but whatever. I talked to him! For twenty whole minutes, even! And he's nicer than I imagined. How can I not have a crush on him?

He holds the door open for me—and I *swoon*.

This is the best day of my life.

TWENTY-ONE

PATRICK

I'm walking into Mr. Day's class when I spot Sara and Joe laughing by her desk. He's leaning in, eyes locked on hers as he focuses on what she's saying, then he grins wide and loudly declares, "I love hot pot too."

Big whoop. Everyone loves hot pot.

I'll admit, this would have been a shocking scene to witness if I hadn't seen them walk into school together. I'd been sitting near the brick wall with Seth and Jimmy, two guys I used to hang out with in middle school, when Joe and Sara strolled up the pathway, completely passing me without a single glance. I even tried to wave to get her attention, but she only had eyes for Joe.

I couldn't believe it. She was talking to him! Walking to school with him! When had they become so chummy? And why hadn't she told me?

So I pulled out my phone and hopped over to her blog, hoping she'd updated it with an explanation, but I was wrong. Not a single update since last week. Normally, she would have texted me everything, then spilled her guts online. But she hadn't even texted me back last night, just left me on Read. It's so unlike her.

Don't I matter to her? What gives?

"Did you see them walk to school together?"

Glancing next to me, I spot Rose standing there. I hadn't even seen her walk over. Her arms are folded, her mouth in a tight line. She looks pissed. Huh. What's weirder is the fact that she's talking to me. I'm not exactly someone Rose keeps in her circle. I'm too loud, too annoying, too immature—at least, that's what her best friend, Mari, told me last year.

As if I care.

Her brown eyes meet mine. "What's the deal with that?"

"I don't know, Rose," I say dryly. "Maybe they're in *love* with each other and we'll get invited to the wedding."

"Ugh, gross. You need to control your girlfriend, Patrick." She flips her shiny hair over her shoulder. I wonder if she practices that move in the mirror. I bet she does. "How can you let her flirt all over the place like that?"

I withhold a snort trying to image Sara flirting—but is that what she's doing right now?

Pushing the thought from my mind, I say, "Lucky for you, she's not my girlfriend." I press my palm against the door frame and lean toward her. "So you know, you and I could always—"

"Ew, Patrick." She wrinkles her nose as she speed walks away from me. "In your dreams."

I follow her into the classroom. I'm about to find my seat when Tammy comes up beside me, nervously fiddling with the end of one of her braided pigtails.

"Wait, I thought Sara was your girlfriend?"

"Are you serious? Tammy, I'm single." I shake my head as I retreat to my desk. "Why can't anyone understand that? Geez."

Once I set my backpack down, I approach Sara's desk. Joe's already wandered over to Rose's seat, and I overhear them discussing Newspaper Club.

"Hey." I rap my knuckles on her desk. "You finished my homework, right?"

"Oh, hey, Patrick!" Her amber eyes shine with excitement. "Guess what happened this morning? You're going to *freak* out. Prepare yourself, I'm serious."

"Good morning, students," Mr. Day says as he strolls through the door. "Please turn in your essays up here at the front, and then we'll begin today's lesson."

A collective shuffling sounds as everyone pulls out their essays.

I stare expectantly at Sara. "Well?"

She cranes her neck to make sure Joe's still chatting with Rose, then says, "Okay, so this morning—"

I'm two seconds away from being fed up. "No, Sara—*my homework*. Did you finish it?"

She gasps, her face paling. My heart stutters, because this reaction tells me everything I need to know.

"Shoot, Patrick," she whispers. "I forgot about your homework."

"*Sara*, agh!"

Whirling away, I slip into my desk and frantically search for a single sheet of paper. How could she do this to me? We agreed she'd do my homework because she lost that stupid bet!

Once I find a pen, I furiously scribble my name at the top.

Then I start writing. Okay, I can do this. My favorite vacation. Where would that be? *Think*, Patrick. The Grand Canyon! Yes! That will have to work.

Sara looms over my shoulder. "Oh! Don't forget to mention the mountains. And the Colorado River, right? Describe its splendor, Patrick! You can do it."

I grit my teeth. This is not helping. My hand cramps, but I keep pushing.

"Any last papers?"

I spring to my feet. "Here!"

Sara's eyes are on me as I race to the front of the room and slap my essay on Mr. Day's desk. So what if it isn't three hundred words? At least I'm turning in *something*.

Mr. Day scrutinizes it. "What's this?"

"Uh—the homework?"

"I asked for a typed paper, Patrick."

My heart sinks. Ugh—Sara! I spin around to glare at her, teeth clenched, and find her fiddling with the hem of her cardigan. An apologetic look crosses her face as I move past her to take my seat, and as Mr. Day begins his lecture, she pulls out her phone.

A second later, my pocket vibrates. I peek at the screen.

Sara: Hey

Sara: Uh, sorry?

Yeah, right. Like she means it! That's a pathetic excuse for an apology. All she cares about is Joe. If I fail English, it's her fault.

Another vibration. I look again.

Sara: Dude, I forgot, okay??

Sara: Why are you so mad?

Sara: I'm sorrryyyyyyy

Sara: That was a stupid bet anyway

I make a gigantic show of turning my phone off, throwing the stink eye at her while I do. Her mouth falls open, eyes narrowing in anger. *Pfft*, what's she mad about? She's the one who's at fault here. So I flit my gaze away and ignore her for the rest of class.

When the bell rings for lunch I don't wait around for her to catch up with me. Sure, it's petty, but I end up sitting at a crowded lunch table to avoid her. There's no room for her to join, but I don't care. I have a right to be mad. Also? The last thing I want to hear is how *cool* and *nice* and *amazing* Joe is. She should have been preoccupied with doing my homework, not focused on stupid Joe. A bet's a bet—and she lost.

Sara looks crestfallen when she realizes there's no room for her at my table, and that's when we both hear it.

"Sara!"

Joe's calling her over to his table, where there's plenty of room for her to join. Rose, Subwayboy, and a few other juniors are sitting around him. I watch Sara's face light up as she slides into the empty space next to him.

I grip my chopsticks so hard I think they may snap. "That traitor's gonna have lunch with Subwayboy?"

I don't realize I've said this aloud until, from next to me, Tammy goes, "Who's Subwayboy?"

"No one," I mumble.

Even though I'm mad at Sara, I'm not going to make her situation worse by telling Tammy that Subwayboy Oliver is now her calculus tutor. That's her own drama to share with Tammy if she wants.

Tammy shrugs. "All right."

I'm surprised Tammy's even speaking to me right now, considering I almost shared a nonconsensual kiss with her yesterday. Ugh, I really shouldn't have done that.

"Hey," I say, and she lifts her eyes to mine. "I'm sorry about trying to kiss you yesterday. That wasn't cool."

The corners of her mouth lift into smile. "Thank you for saying that," she says.

Across from us, Joe's eyes crinkle as he laughs at something Sara says. I can tell she's sharing a story by the way she's waving her hands around, something she does when she's excited. So now Joe gets all her attention?

"What, are they best friends now or something?" I grumble.

Tammy's eyes dart from me to Sara as she smooths her napkin in her lap. "I mean, they seem pretty cool?"

Listen, I'm well aware I should be grateful Tammy's letting me sit with her, but validating Sara and Joe's friendship? Not. Helping.

"Don't say that." I pull my tray closer and shoot her a sidelong look. "Eat your lunch, Tammy. It's the most important meal of the day."

Tammy only throws me an inquisitive look. "I thought that was breakfast?"

But I barely hear her.

Sara's not replacing me.

She's *not.*

TWENTY-TWO

SARA

Here's what's going on inside my brain: I'm sitting next to Joe, *yippee*!

And also: But I'm directly across from Subwayboy, *whyyyyyyy meeeee*!

Rose sits on the other side of Joe and, oddly, Lulu's at the end of our table. That's strange. She's not with her artsy friends today. Lulu is mysterious, though, so who knows why she does anything. She gives me a low nod of acknowledgment, so I toss her a wave.

And then I understand why this very specific group of people are sitting together.

"We were talking about the first Newspaper Club meeting after school," Joe tells me. "Think you can make it?"

Oliver's eyes jump to mine as he shovels rice into his mouth. The last thing I want is to spend lunch being scrutinized by him, so I focus on his brother.

"Oh—you're all in newspaper?"

"Yeah, it's been a little tough," Joe admits, then gestures to Rose. "We didn't get many applications, but we still had enough interest to form this group."

"I don't think people wanted to write an extra essay," Rose adds, sparing a cool glance my way. "So we had to settle with you, Lulu, and these three juniors."

I blink at her. Wait, I'm in the club?

And, hold on, did she say three *juniors*?!

Oliver's watching me, one eyebrow raised. He chews in silence, slow and deliberate, as if waiting for me to say something. Next to him, a shorter boy with round glasses and dark, neatly combed hair perks up, his lips splitting into an overeager grin. He's sitting beside a girl with light-brown skin and rose-gold hair, two cute space buns on either side of her head. She swallows her bite of tofu, then smiles at me.

Oliver should really take notes.

"So you're all"—I point to everyone across from me—"juniors?"

"Yeah, so?"

There's a challenge in Oliver's tone. I'm about to respond when Lulu chooses this very moment to interject.

"I'm not. I'm whatever I choose to be." She keeps a completely straight face as she picks up her juice and takes a long, slow sip, not breaking eye contact with me—not even when she sets the can down. "I'm all the grades."

Uh, okay, Lulu.

"Nice to meet you! I'm Mickey Dean."

The overeager boy next to Oliver shoots his arm out, extending his hand toward me and, in the process, knocks over Oliver's soda. Oliver steadies the can before it spills.

"Well, actually, my name is Michael. But everyone just calls me Mickey. You're Sara Lin, right? I read your article!" He keeps shaking my hand, our arms moving up and down as his words run together. "It's such an honor to be in a club with seniors! I promise we'll work superhard, right, Oliver?"

Joe and I exchange a quick glance, and I can tell he's trying to withhold a laugh. Rose just cups her chin in her hand, huffy and indignant.

Oliver's focused on scooping more rice onto his spoon. "Sure."

"And I'm Cordelia," the girl beside Mickey Dean says, beaming brightly. She has a swipe of shimmery highlighter on her cheeks that looks dazzling when it catches the light. "It's so great to meet you."

Eager anticipation swirls within me. They're so *nice*. I can't believe I haven't crossed paths with them before. But it's fine, because now I get to work with them—which means I get to work with Joe.

Ah! More time with Joe!

I have to stop myself from swooning right here and now.

"Wow, it's really great to meet you," I say earnestly. "I'm excited to officially join."

When lunch ends, Joe tells me where we're meeting after school, and my stomach does a double backflip in anticipation. He walks with me to our next class, but I can hardly concentrate as we sit through our history lesson, followed by science and calculus. All I can think about is Newspaper Club.

That—and Oliver.

I mean, he's a junior! I should have put it together this morning when Joe said *little brother*. However, I was too stunned from A) realizing Joseph Yang lives right across the hall from me and B) processing that Joe and Oliver are actually related.

It gives me a confidence boost. Ha! To think I was intimidated by Oliver this *entire time*. He's just a kid. A silly little junior one grade below me. I have a whole entire year of education stored up in my brain that he doesn't have yet. So take that, Subwayboy.

But, ugh. He's probably going to yell at me again for not prioritizing my studies. I mean, Mr. Day's walking us through an equation right now and I haven't been paying him the teeniest bit of attention.

Oliver and I are supposed to meet in the library after school today, but I'll see him in Newspaper Club instead. Is he going to be upset that I joined? Even Patrick thought it wasn't a good idea.

Oh! Right. Patrick!

I twist in my seat right as the bell rings. Without so much as a single look in my direction, Patrick flies to his feet, grabs his backpack from the floor, and flees the classroom.

It's okay. I can catch up.

"Hey, Patrick!"

He picks up his pace—even though I *know* he heard me. The stinker.

I seize my shoulder bag next to my desk and hurry after him, trying to think of the right thing to say, but as soon as I launch out the door, I run straight into Lulu.

Stumbling back, I catch myself on the wall behind me. Once I've regained my bearings, I blink down the hall, but Patrick's already disappeared.

"Geez, Lulu. You've got to stop doing that."

She follows my gaze, her body falling eerily still. As if she's imitating a statue. "I wouldn't worry about him if I were you," she says in this ominous tone. "He'll come around. He always does—unlike the subway. It stops coming around after midnight, right?"

My reaction is visceral, arms jerking back as my eyes widen. "Wait, what did you just say?"

She sighs, like I'm somehow both unreasonable *and* a distraction. "Sara Lin, I'm late for a tarot appointment. The cards won't read themselves."

As she turns away, I clasp my hand around her wrist. "Hold on, why'd you bring up the subway? Did Patrick tell you something?"

I swear, if Patrick's retaliating by spreading the Subwayboy story, I'm going to have a few choice words for him. I mean, if he keeps blabbing to everyone, then Subwayboy will eventually find out.

I can't let that happen.

Her eyes linger on my hand, then she slowly drags her gaze up until her silver contacts bore into my eyes. "Tell me what?"

This time I lightly grasp her shoulders and gently shake her, whispering, "About the most embarrassing moment of my life."

Lulu isn't fazed. Because of course she isn't.

"No." She takes a giant step backward. "But doesn't everyone already know? Secrets are a heavy burden to carry, Sara Lin. So, I leave you with a freeing spell."

Before I have a chance to react, she swoops her arms into two huge circles—like she's imitating a windmill—and then brings them together in a thunderclap above her head.

"Uh, hey?"

Tammy has suddenly appeared by my side, looking between me and Lulu, as if attempting to decipher what the heck is happening in the hallway. Lulu only levels her eyes on mine, bringing her arms down by her sides.

"Liberty awaits you, Sara Lin," Lulu says, then draws her attention to Tammy. "Ready to go, Tammy Yokoyama?"

"Yup," Tammy says, all chipper and optimism. "See you tomorrow, Sara!"

As they walk off, I'm left in a cloud of confusion. What on *earth* was that about? What does Lulu mean everyone already knows? She must be kidding—right? Or does that mean Subwayboy knows too?

Ugh, I really hope this is all just Lulu nonsense. There's no way Oliver remembers the night in the subway. We ate lunch together today, for crying out loud. He's seen my face too many times since our last tutoring session, including this morning on our walk to school, and *every* time we lock eyes, he glares back at me with that bored look of disdain.

If he recognized me, I would know. I'm sure of it.

I check the time on my phone. Shoot! If I don't hustle, I'm going to be late for the first Newspaper Club meeting. And I can't let that happen. Not if I'm going to get my act together and focus on my priorities, because newspaper *is* a priority. Won't it look good on my college applications? Isn't it a school activity?

Okay, so what if Joe is part of the club? And maybe the perfect someone to grant me my first kiss? It just means everything's working out in my favor, that's all. A tiny coincidence.

Bring on the romance, universe. I'm *ready*.

TWENTY-THREE

SARA

I'm popping around the corner—with a quickened merriment in my step, might I add—when I spot Oliver sitting in an empty chair outside the journalism room. A silent gasp escapes through my lips. Quickly backtracking, I press my back against the wall and stifle a groan.

He's the last person I want to see right now. Also, why is he sitting there all mysterious like that? Sure, he's reading a book—so it's not *that* odd—but why is he all alone?

Is Lulu right? Does he know something? Maybe he's waiting to confront me, but the subway incident feels like it happened forever ago. No reason for me to ever bring it up again. I'd go as far to say it's water under the bridge. It's yesterday's peanut butter sandwich. Is that a saying? If not, maybe I should make it one.

Here's what I do know: it's time to start fresh. Oliver's only a junior. A *junior*! It's laughable, really, thinking back to how nervous I was around him. In reality, I'm his elder. His senior. He *must* respect me.

Straightening my shoulders, I hold my head high as I step around the corner.

"Oliver Yang."

At the sound of his name, he looks up. When he sees that it's just me, his face falls like he's just been summoned to detention.

"What?"

"Uh." So, I hadn't given much thought as to what I'd say next. "Why aren't you in the meeting?"

He checks his watch. Interesting. Who wears watches these days?

"It doesn't start for another five minutes."

"Oh." My eyes drop to the floor. "Right."

Assuming that's all I've come to ask, he goes back to his book. Which means I'm left standing there, arms crossed, losing confidence by the second. *C'mon, Sara. Don't let him get to you.*

I clear my throat. "So—that thing I found out. Crazy, huh? I can't believe I didn't realize."

Oliver heaves a long sigh, green eyes entangling with mine. "What are you on about? Just say it."

"It's just crazy," I continue, a bite of determination layered in my voice now, "you're a *junior.*"

He makes a show of shutting his book. "Of all the things you found out about me today, *that's* the most shocking to you?" He rolls his eyes. "What, you thought I was a senior or something?"

"I mean, I'm a senior and they assigned a junior to tutor me." I brave moving a few steps closer to where he sits. "Kinda weird, right?"

Oliver slides his book in his backpack before lifting his

eyes to meet mine. "Sure, I guess it's weird," he says dully. "You must be embarrassed to find out you're being tutored by a junior who also happens to be your next-door neighbor."

At this, my face flames. "What's embarrassing about that? Who's embarrassed here? Why would I even—?"

Oliver's on his feet now, his full height towering over me as he leans in closer. "Really, Sara Lin?" There's a teasing, knowing edge in his tone. "Nothing to be embarrassed about—nothing at all lurking around your head?"

"What?" My feet act on autopilot, as if sensing I should now put distance between us. "What are you—are you talking about—? The, uh—?"

My heart beats faster, so fast that it feels like I've consumed ten energy drinks. His eyebrows do that Oliver thing where they draw together as he examines me.

There's no way he's referring to the subway incident, right? Not after all this time? But I can't tell, because he keeps his stare level with mine. Nothing in his eyes gives anything away, which is even more infuriating.

"God, what are you staring at?" I smooth my skirt to give my hands something to do. "All I'm saying is that I'm a year older than you, so you need to show me some respect."

"Are you *serious*?" He tilts his head, golden hair flopping to the left as he does. "You think *I'm* the problem here?"

"I just mean sometimes you come off as rude," I explain, suddenly exhausted by this topic. "But I guess we both have to work on . . ."

I trail off, not because I can't think of anything to say, but because he's turned his back on me. And now he's strutting away—during the middle of our conversation!

"Maybe when you're better at math, we'll see," he tosses over his shoulder.

He hasn't gone far, lingering outside the journalism classroom. It doesn't take long for me to catch up to him.

"See!" I fling a hand his way. "That's *exactly* what I'm talking about."

"Respect has nothing to do with age, Sara Lin. It has to be earned." His face shifts, like he's just remembered something. "Oh, you wanna reschedule tutoring since we have this meeting?"

Earned? What is he even talking about? He should respect me because I'm older, not because I have to earn it by being his friend or something. Geez, doesn't he know anything?

Irritation flits through me. "Are you kidding? No, I don't want to reschedule—*ever*."

"All right." He shrugs, truly indifferent, then jiggles the handle to the classroom. "Good luck with your test."

The doorknob doesn't turn. He tries again, this time putting more force behind his tug.

"Fine, *whatever*." I cross my arms as I watch him struggle. "What are you doing? Just open it."

He pulls harder, but it doesn't budge. "I *am* trying."

"Let me try." I attempt to step in front of him as I reach for the handle, but he blocks my path with his body.

"Stop reaching." He swats my hand away. "It won't open."

This only makes me want to try again, so I do. "What if I can open it? And don't sneer at me like that. I'm your senior, remember?"

"That actually means nothing to me," he says flatly, still blocking my path.

I manage to slip my hand by him. When it lands on the doorknob, I'm able to tug for a brief second before his elbow nudges me aside. Well, that settles it. The door *is* locked.

"Argh—just knock, then, you stupid *Subwayboy*."

The words roll off my tongue before I can stop them. Oliver freezes in place, his eyes locking on mine. Heat flushes into my cheeks.

Oh no—did he catch that?

"Hey."

I'm so grateful for this interruption that I could spontaneously combust with joy. We whirl toward the voice. Lulu's poked her head out from the classroom behind us, inching the door wider.

"You're trying to open the wrong door." She looks between us, silver eyes shifting back and forth. "Are you coming to the meeting or what?"

TWENTY-FOUR

SARA

There's a lingering scent of turkey sandwiches and pencil shavings in this classroom, and I wonder if the journalism instructor eats lunch in here by himself. This is not what I should be focused on, though. Rose has been breaking down what our meetings will look like this year and what she'll expect from us, and I've sort of tuned her out. Because I've been fixated on if Oliver—and if he put the pieces together.

From beside me, Joe scribbles important details in his spiral notebook. I spare a sidelong glance at Oliver, who watches with narrowed eyes as Rose paces back and forth as she speaks at the front of the classroom. That familiar bored expression plays across his features. Does anything in this great wild world entertain him? We should sooner expect a solar eclipse than a smile from him. I mean, if he's so unenthused by the idea of writing for the newspaper, why is he even here?

And the bigger question: Has Oliver known about me this entire time? I'm going to feel like an enormous doofus if that's the case. Because why wouldn't he say anything? Maybe he was waiting for me to bring it up. Ugh, good thing he's not my tutor anymore. I can't imagine any more one-on-one time with him.

"So Joe and Oliver are going to report on the festival," Mari says from beside Rose. She's the club's vice president, I learned earlier, and is in charge of making sure we all meet our deadlines. "Lulu, you good with focusing on horoscopes?"

"Always," Lulu intones.

I cock my head. How did Lulu even get to the journalism classroom so fast? I thought she had a tarot reading. Weird. But I guess that's Lulu. So mysterious.

"Great," Mari says, beaming. "Cordelia and Mickey Dean, are you good with graphics and editing?"

"Yes, ma'am." Mickey gives a polished salute. "Forever and ever prepared. You can expect nothing but the best from these two humble, hardworking juniors. We promise to deliver through blood, sweat, and tears. We shall conquer! We shall be victorious! We—"

Cordelia puts a gentle arm on his shoulder and Mickey, who did not seem to notice he'd risen from his seat during his impassioned speech, sits back down.

"Okay, got it. Thanks, Mickey Dean," Rose says as she marks something down in her notes. "Moving on."

I wonder if Oliver's noticed how *respectful* Mickey Dean's being to his seniors. As one should act. This is the high-school hierarchy, after all.

Mickey points two thumbs to the sky. "Yes, my queen. I'll shut up now."

Rose closes her notebook as Mari says, "Everyone's clear with their assignments, then?"

Everyone nods. Except me. Because I don't have an assignment. They forgot about me, which is mortifying, because I'm sitting right here.

"Um," I pipe up. "What about me?"

Oliver leans forward and gives me a pointed look. Geez, who poured spoiled milk in his cereal? I'm not sure how to interpret this. Does he think I don't deserve an assignment? Well, he's wrong. I'm a great writer. And I'm going to prove it.

"Sara Lin, clueless as always." Rose opens her notebook once again, leaning over to jot something down. "Why didn't you say anything?"

Uh, hello? I'm saying something now.

I don't say that aloud, though.

She sighs, heavy and dramatic, like I am a massive zit she's just discovered on her chin. "We're gonna have to rearrange everything so we can fit another article in for you."

"Oh, we don't want to do that," Joe says, brightening. "Sara, why don't you come with me and Oliver to the festival? We could use the extra help."

I sit up a little straighter, my eyes meeting his. "Okay, sounds great."

Two overlapping voices shout, "No!"

Rose and Oliver look like we've proposed changing our uniform color to highlighter yellow. Extreme displeasure is apparent on their faces.

"Why not?" I push back, summoning courage to stand up for myself. "I mean, I'd have to get my dad's permission to go to the festival, but I'd love to write about it."

"Of course. We'll figure it out. Don't worry," Joe says encouragingly.

Oliver drops his face into his hands, the motion sending his glasses up his forehead and into his thick hair. Wow, say you don't want to be around me without *saying* it, Subwayboy.

I choose to ignore this overreaction. "You think so? I mean, it'll depend on my grades, but—"

"Wait, wait. Is there really a need for this?"

Rose is miffed now, because we're not following her leadership. And that's the thing she enjoys most. Being in charge. Bossing people around.

"Lulu, weren't you, uh. Weren't you saying you needed more people for your"—Rose tries to think of the word—"spells section?"

Lulu folds one hand over the other, completely unnerved by Rose's desire to get her way. "Never."

"Actually, Rose, I think the festival may be our best option," Mari jumps in. "It's going to be big this year, so it's better to have more reporters on the ground. That way we get more coverage."

It's clear Rose isn't happy about this. As she frowns, a satisfactory thrill shoots through me. Because, wow—I actually stood up for myself in front of her. I've never done that before today.

Also? Ha! See? I'm needed at the festival. Rose can't stop me from contributing to this club.

"Fine. If we need more people, I guess I'll have to join too." Rose points her pen at Lulu. "Looks like you're gonna have to take care of those spells by yourself."

"Always," Lulu agrees ominously.

"It's settled, then." Rose places her hands on her hips, as though this superhero stance allows her to regain her power.

"It'll be me, Joe, Oliver, and Sara at the festival. Everyone okay with that?"

Oliver hangs his head, rubbing at his temples like this idea is giving him a massive headache. Joe, on the other hand, gives two enthusiastic thumbs-up. I go on pretending like Oliver does not exist in my world, and it's a much happier place because of this.

"Sounds excellent," Joe insists, green eyes gleaming as he smiles at me.

Tha-thump, tha-thump goes my heart. *Eeee*, I have plans with Joe! Well, and his brother. And Rose. But still! Joe is in the mix, and that's not nothing—especially if I'm going to get to know him better. This is my big opportunity. It's everything I could want, so I *have* to make sure I don't blow it.

Rose only smirks. "Can't wait."

TWENTY-FIVE

SARA

A week later, Vicky and I grab boba after school.

I haven't hung out with her since my birthday, which feels like a million years ago. It's rare she doesn't have to work today, so I cherish this time with her. There's so much I need to tell her—stuff I haven't even had time to write about on my blog—so I start by filling her in on my fight with Patrick.

Yes, we're still not talking. But it's not like I haven't tried. Patrick's so stubborn, it's childish. Did he *really* expect me to do his homework? I barely do my own homework most days. That's why he should've had a plan B. Or a plan C or D, for that matter.

Vicky stays neutral whenever Patrick and I get into disagreements, and it's no different this time. She tells me to apologize for real, because it's clear our friendship is bigger than a homework assignment. And she's right, of course. Because she's always right about these things.

It's times like these I wish Vicky and I went to the same

school, but she goes to Brookside High, a public school closer to her neighborhood. When I asked Dad if I could go there for high school, he said no. Brookside is in a different school district from us, an entire twenty-minute subway ride away. I can walk to Eagle Gate in ten minutes. Seven, if I walk fast.

I like the Brookside uniforms more, though. They're deep maroon and gold instead of navy and silver, and when I told Dad those colors were more flattering on me, he laughed like I'd told a joke before saying, *Oh, you're serious? Sara, uniform color isn't a good reason to pick a school.*

But imagine if Vicky went to Eagle Gate and joined Newspaper Club with me. We'd have so much fun! Then I remember she has her job at Kiki's, so it'd be an unlikely scenario. Still, a girl can dream.

Vicky's always been good with money, unlike me, who makes silly bets and spends the rest on hot pot. She's saving for college, which is why she works so many hours. I haven't thought that far. About college, I mean. Although I really should, seeing as it's our senior year.

After Vicky fills me in on her classes and the funny work drama she's not involved in but hears about anyway, I tell her about my tiff with Oliver—specifically how I don't have a tutor anymore.

Vicky's dark, glossy hair shifts in the breeze as we walk. "Subwayboy *for sure* remembers it was you?"

"You should have seen his face," I say, then take another sip from my drink. Brown sugar boba, my favorite. "His reaction was so obvious, which probably means he knew all along but never said anything."

"Well, that's a jerk move. Why wouldn't he say anything?"

"Ugh, I don't know. I guess I never said anything either—but who cares. All I know is I need a tutor."

Vicky thinks for several seconds, stirring her strawberry boba around with the thick straw. "Patrick can't help?"

"I told you, we're fighting." Then I try my best to make big doe eyes at her. "That's why I need you, my prettiest, smartest, kindest cousin ever."

"I'll help you, no need for all the flattery." She laughs.

Vicky's also taking calculus at Brookside and, I hope, absorbing more than me. Which is perfect, because this proves I don't even need Subwayboy anymore. Take that!

"How long do you plan on fighting with Patrick?" she asks, all casual.

"*Ugh*, it's not like I wanted to make him mad, Vicky." I slurp the last of my drink. "I tried apologizing. He's just stubborn—I don't know what's gotten into him lately."

Vicky gives me a sidelong glance, as if telepathically reminding me I should offer him a real apology.

"*Anyway*," I say, moving on. "I've got bigger problems right now."

"At least you'll get to go to the school festival with Joe. That's good, right?"

"True."

After my first Newspaper Club meeting, I texted Vicky to tell her about the festival and how I'd get to hang out with Joe if I went, since we're supposed to interview students together. She was so excited for me. Not about the Joe part (although that still is a big bonus), but about my writing. She said this was a great way to start letting more people read my work, and how brave is that? I'd never let anyone besides her and Patrick read my blog, so her encouragement meant a lot.

Vicky peels off the sidewalk and stops under a forest-green awning. I follow her, noticing we've temporarily paused at the corner store.

"I have to run in here real quick," she insists. "Mom asked me to grab some stuff for her."

"Then after we'll study for calculus? I have so much to learn, I'm *hopeless*."

She releases a gentle tinkling laugh. "Just wait out here, I won't be long."

After she disappears inside, I find a nearby trash can and toss my empty boba cup inside. Then I slump onto a bench outside the store, right near the big glass window.

Pulling out my phone, I navigate to my conversation with Patrick and read what I'd last sent him. The apology texts I'd fired off in Mr. Day's class. They do seem insincere now that I read them back, so it's no wonder he still hasn't replied.

Should I send another? No, he probably doesn't want to hear from me. I don't get why he's so sensitive about this. It's not like that essay was a huge part of our grade.

When Vicky doesn't emerge after a few minutes, I whirl around and peek inside. What's taking so long? It takes me a moment to spot her standing near an endcap displaying canned lima beans—currently on sale, apparently—and then I realize she's laughing. Huh? Are the lima beans doing stand-up comedy? Only, no—she's laughing because she's *talking* to someone.

I rise to my feet and head inside, excusing my way past customers until I find her.

And that's when I see him.

Joe.

My heart stutters. Joe and Vicky are midconversation between the lima beans and mosquito spray, and of course Joe looks perfect. He's still in his school uniform, hair perfectly coifed, hands gripping a bright-red shopping basket filled with pantry items.

"Oh, Sara." Vicky waves me over. "Sorry I'm taking so long!"

Joe grins at me. "Hey, Sara."

Vicky looks between us. "Wait, you know my cousin?"

I widen my eyes, attempting to telepathically tell her that this is The Joe.

"Yes! Sara's in my class," Joe says. "I had no idea she's your cousin. What a small world."

Vicky laughs. "It really is."

"I quite literally bumped into Vicky while looking for chicken broth," Joe fills me in, his eyes lingering on her before meeting mine. "We used to go to Brookside together before I transferred." He points a finger at her. "I knew you looked familiar."

"We had some classes together, but never really talked," Vicky adds. "I do remember you, though."

"I definitely remember you." Joe says this in his overly friendly way, and it reminds me why I like him so much. He's so sweet to everyone.

"So funny seeing you here," I say.

His phone chimes. When he glances at it, his face drops. "Shoot, I have to go. I'm making dinner for my little brother."

What, Subwayboy can't cook? That's cute. Maybe this is the one thing he isn't good at.

"Nice running into you, Vicky," Joe goes on. "Oh, by the

way, Sara and I are going to our school festival next week. You should come! It's on Friday."

And then my world goes all hazy and dreamlike, because he *clasps* his *hand* on my *shoulder*.

Ahhhh! My stomach may just burst into a thousand butterflies!

That doesn't happen, though. Instead, I nod along as a blush rises in my cheeks.

"Sounds perfect." Vicky tucks her hair behind her ear as Joe releases his hand. (*Nooo!* I was appreciating that hand on my shoulder!) "Count me in."

"Great, see you both there."

Leaving us with one final dazzling smile, he heads to the checkout counter.

Vicky giggles and pretends to fan herself, and, giggling along with her, I pull her around the corner so we're both out of sight.

"I can't believe you've been telling me about Joseph Yang the whole time and I didn't know," Vicky whispers.

From over the aisle, I spot the cashier bagging Joe's haul. "Wait, so you know him?"

"I'd seen him around school when he went to Brookside, but we never talked or anything," she says. "Wow, you're right. He's so nice!"

My heart warms at her approval. It's kind of exciting to have a crush. When I first started to like Patrick, I'd get this excited tingle in my stomach every time I was in his presence. Thank goodness that doesn't happen anymore since we're just friends.

Now I've started to get it again whenever I'm talking to

Joe, which, as it turns out, is a lot. If we leave for school at the same time, we'll walk over together and chat the entire way there. And since Patrick still isn't talking to me, I've started sitting with Joe and the Newspaper Club at lunch. We've only had one more newspaper meeting, and even though Oliver and Rose were there, I got to help map out which student programs we'd try to interview at the festival. My belly does a little flip every time he smiles at me.

To invite Vicky to the festival with us? That's just another example of his generosity. Always thinking of others, like how he's making dinner for Subwayboy. I mean, can he get any more perfect?

I doubt it.

TWENTY-SIX

SARA

"*Vicky*," I moan, flopping back on my carpeted bedroom floor. "I thought you said you were good at calculus."

"I *am* good at calculus," she insists, tucking her pencil behind her ear. "It's not my fault you're not understanding anything."

"I can't do this anymore." I fling one arm over my eyes. It's overdramatic, but whatever. Math turns me into a dramatic person. "We're not getting anywhere."

It's nearing eight o'clock and we've only managed to study half of what I need to know for my pretest tomorrow. The upside? It's a practice exam to help us prepare for our real test. The downside? I haven't retained any information from tonight's study session. And it's not for lack of trying. I'm not distracted by Oliver or Joe or anything. I'm simply not understanding this.

If you're wondering why I've never asked my accountant, good-at-math father for help with calculus, it's because he's the worst tutor in the world. Seriously, some people are not born to teach, and that man is one of them.

I made the mistake of asking him to explain algebra a few years ago, and he expected me to *just get it*. Um, that's not how my brain works. So our session ended with him tugging at his moustache in great frustration and me crying into my hands. And once he saw how upset I was, he scooped us two giant bowls of ice cream and insisted we watch this Fleetwood Mac documentary until I felt better. It honestly helped ease the tension, but since then I've been on my own when it comes to math homework.

"I should be the one complaining here," Vicky mumbles.

"My life is over. Now I'll never get to go to the festival with Joe, which means I'll never get my first kiss from him. I'm going to die a Virgin Lips, never having known the sweet, *sweet* feeling of his tender soft mouth against mine." I peek from behind my arm. "Why did I have to be born bad at math?"

"Quit being so dramatic." Vicky rolls onto her shins. "This test doesn't even count."

"For the thousandth time, Victoria." I sit up and look at her. "Did you not hear my father when he said I could never go out again if I failed one more test? That includes a pretest."

She's already started packing her things. "Sorry, Sara. It's getting late, but I've marked all the formulas on the study sheet for you. If you at least memorize those, you should do okay."

"Wait, Vicky—"

As she heads toward my bedroom door, I leap to my feet, but she's already slinging her backpack over her shoulders.

"Hey, maybe try making amends with Oliver?" She

suggests as she opens my door. "Even if it's awkward, he seems like a really good tutor."

I pout, puffing out my lower lip, hoping this display will make her want to stay. It doesn't. Instead, she laughs and says, "Good luck, girl. You can do this."

Once she leaves, I pace around my room. Ugh! It's useless. What am I going to do?

Well, I can at least buckle up and try. Vicky told me to memorize these formulas, which I can do. Easy! I don't need stupid Subwayboy for that. What if I stay up late and teach myself the rest? Maybe he'll come to *me* for tutoring. That'll show him.

Except—well. It doesn't go well.

Dad comes in a little after ten o'clock and tells me I need to get a good night's rest, and even though I sleep okay, I'm nervous the next day when I step into Mr. Day's classroom and take the pretest.

Since it's so early in the school year, Mr. Day's only using this test to see how much we've retained so far, but still. The equations and formulas swim before my eyes, blurring together. I hear Oliver's voice in my head, saying, *Convergent or divergent? Which is it, Sara Lin?*

I have no idea.

Our results are posted on the bulletin board outside Mr. Day's class after lunch. Students congregate in the hall as they check their marks, but I hang back until the crowd clears. The test was difficult, but I did manage to memorize some formulas. Did I use them correctly? That's the real question.

So far, the reactions seem excited. Someone even says, "That was easier than I expected!"

Maybe I didn't do as bad as I thought?

The bell rings. People scurry to their next class, and I seize the opportunity when no one else is around to check the board. I scan down columns of names until I find mine.

SARA LIN: 32%

A gasp sticks in my throat. That can't be right, can it? This is the worst grade I've ever gotten in my entire history of school. Why is it so low? Did I really bomb that badly?

Ugh, what was I thinking? Subwayboy knows what he's talking about when it comes to calculus. I just need to focus on retaining the information. But, geez, how embarrassing is this grade printed here for all to see? Why does Mr. Day do this? Hasn't he ever heard of emailing grades? I guess that's too much work, but whatever.

I refuse to let this awful grade sit here for all to see, so I reach into my shoulder bag and peel a tiny piglet sticker from a sticker sheet and cover up the offending grade.

I've *failed.* Worse, I'm going to have to tell Dad, which means no school festival.

My life is over.

TWENTY-SEVEN

PATRICK

I'm not a complex guy, really. All I want is a sincere apology from Sara. I don't think that's too much to ask.

As I walk through the school doors the next morning, I wonder if today is the day Sara comes to this realization herself. It's been over a week since we last spoke. This is the longest we've gone without talking aside from the time she went on vacation with her dad and accidentally dropped her phone in the ocean, which she said made her feel like "a prairie girl" since she had no technological means of communication.

I'd be lying if I said I didn't miss her.

I'm extra-early, which means there aren't a ton of students around. Am I secretly hoping Sara's early, too, and that she'll approach me with an apology? Maybe. But I don't spot her anywhere.

I do, however, find her tutor when I round the corner to get to my locker. There's no one else in this wing. Huh. I wonder why he's also early.

"Hey, Sara's tutor."

He glances over his shoulder and, upon recognizing me, arranges his face into a look of utter annoyance. Without a single word he resumes digging through his locker. Pretty rude, if you ask me. What did I ever do to him?

"You're here early." Then, just to get under his skin, I say, "Avoiding someone?"

His head jerks in my direction, clearly caught off guard. "What? Uh—no."

"C'mon, I know you're Sara's neighbor," I say, cutting through his white lie. "She tells me everything, although we're kind of going through a rough patch right now. She was supposed to do me a favor, but then she forgot and it really screwed me over."

Oliver shoves a textbook in his locker. *Hard*. Metal rattles, echoing through the empty hall.

"Anyway, I'm trying to figure out how to make amends with her," I go on. "I don't want to just let it go, you know? So I'm hoping she'll apologize—"

"Why are you telling me all this?"

"Well, since you're her tutor and you spend so much time together, I was hoping maybe you'd talk to her."

Did this plan form in my mind the minute I saw him standing here alone? Yes. Will I admit that to him? Never.

Oliver slams his locker then whirls around to face me, mouth flat. "Nope. No way. No. Stop involving me in your weird relationship problem. I've got enough going on already. Figure it out on your own."

I scoff then slide my backpack straps off my shoulders. No wonder Sara called tutoring a nightmare. This guy's the worst.

"What are you even *talking* about? When have we ever involved you, dude?"

He tugs his backpack on, glaring at me from behind those glasses he always wears. "I'm not an idiot. I remember you two from the subway station."

My heart lurches in my chest. I'm too shocked to immediately lob a snarky reply, but it doesn't matter, because he's already walking away.

"Why—wait, *what*?" I splutter. "I mean, what subway station? I've never even been there! I don't know what a subway is!"

Oliver rounds the corner, disappearing from sight. And here I am looking foolish, calling out to nobody. Huh, I guess he knew all along. There's nothing I can do about that now.

Oh boy, I can't wait to see the look on Sara's face when she finds out about this.

Except she won't. Because we're not talking.

And if I told her that Subwayboy knows *she's* the girl who came up and asked to kiss him, she'd get really upset. She'd been trying so hard to hide her identity and then, when she finally worked up the courage to tell him, she couldn't. Even though we're not speaking, I don't want her to feel miserable. Besides, she's been distracted by the wrong things lately. This is another unnecessary distraction, kind of like our fight.

Have I even crossed her mind in the last few days? Surely I have. She must miss me, right? Not that I want her to miss me.

Except, don't I want that? Hasn't it been torture seeing her eat lunch with Joe?

Oh man. What's wrong with me? This is so stupid.

I spin my locker combination and right as I'm throwing

open the door, I'm bombarded with an avalanche of—valentines? Gasping in shock, I leap back. Out topples confetti hearts and flower petals and sweet-smelling envelopes sealed with heart-shaped stickers.

What the heck? Is this a joke?

I collect the mess into a pile on the floor, reaching for heart-shaped note the size of a textbook. There's no name written on the front, but there *is* one thing—

Your anonymous lover.

TWENTY-EIGHT

PATRICK

So, two things are clear. One: I have a secret admirer. And two: I have no idea who they are, hence the "secret" aspect.

But I'm going to find out.

After lunch I get to class early to do some sleuthing. I'm at my desk, rapping my fingertips on the flat surface, trying my best to surreptitiously glance around the room.

Who the heck would leave me love letters?

My eyes flit to Mari, but no. Unlikely. She's Rose's best friend, and if Rose doesn't approve of me, Mari certainly won't.

What about Jessica? Hmm, doubtful. Yesterday she told me I was ugly.

Tammy? *Nah*, she totally hates me. I mean, she's been nice to me at lunch, but that's only after I apologized for trying to kiss her. Mostly, I think she feels bad for me because Sara and I aren't talking.

Is it Hannah? Right now she's giggling at something

Marcus said, leaning in closer. The likely observation is that she's into *him*, not me.

And that's when Sara Lin walks into class, head hung low and shoulders slouched. Her mouth does that little wavering thing, which only happens when she's really upset.

Could Sara be my secret admirer? Is this her way of trying to apologize? But if so, why does she look so down in the dumps?

Instead of heading to her desk, she approaches Joe. He greets her with a friendly wave—why is that guy always in a good mood?—before registering something's wrong. And now Sara's revealing something to him, talking with her hands. I can't make out what she's saying. All of a sudden, she covers her face and begins to cry.

Oh snap. Is she crying because she put all those love letters in my locker and I haven't even acknowledged her grand gesture?

Joe lays a comforting hand on her shoulder. Sara's tears only come faster.

What on *earth*? Sure, we're in a little fight over some stupid bet, but *what* did I miss? Maybe I've misinterpreted things. Sara's not my admirer. Clearly, she has a crush on Joe, and what if she told him about her crush? Now he's turning her down in the middle of class. Right in front of everyone!

Ugh, if he hurt her, I'm going to make sure he pays.

I march over to them just in time to hear Joe say, "It's okay, we'll figure something out. Why don't you come over tonight and I can—"

That's it. I slam my palm on his desk. The motion startles them. Sara's head snaps in my direction, confusion playing behind her eyes.

Apologies don't matter right now. She needs a friend, and I'm her *best* friend. I'll make this right. Move over, Joe. She doesn't need you, anyway.

"Everything's fine, Sara. Stop crying. I've decided to forgive you for everything you've done."

She gives me a watery smile. "Patrick?"

I raise my eyebrows as if to say, *Um, yeah?*

And then she throws her arms around me.

"You're finally talking to me again! I'm *so* sorry for being a total jerk—you have no idea what I've been through. I wanted to call you yesterday but I didn't because I know how you can get, and then I freaking *failed* my calculus test because I suck so bad."

She squeezes my torso tighter and—what is happening to me? All I can smell is the sweet scent of her peach shampoo and, for some reason, it makes my heart beat faster. My hands fold around her, passing along comfort before I realize we're hugging in the middle of the classroom—something we've never done before—and push her away from me.

"Okay, okay. Calm down. I got it. I forgive you, okay? I just wanted to know why this guy"—I gesture at Joe—"is making you cry? Unless you were actually upset about me, which is totally cool—"

"Oh, no! She wasn't—I didn't—" Joe stammers. He collects himself when her head swivels toward him. "Sara, I was just about to suggest that you study at my place tonight. Do you think that would help?"

Sara lights up like a comet in the night sky. "Really? You'd do that for me?"

"Of course," Joe insists. "Whatever it takes to get your dad's permission to come to the festival."

I'm so confused. What is happening?

"Wow, thank you so much. I'll come tonight."

Then Sara reaches out and shakes his hand in this oddly professional way. I think she's just nervous.

But now I'm really confused. I thought Oliver was her tutor? Now Joe's tutoring her? What happened in the time we weren't talking? Surely Sara didn't tell Oliver about the subway incident. If she did, it *would* explain why she's now avoiding him. Maybe he took it badly and told her he couldn't tutor her anymore. Ugh, that little punk!

As Joe slides into his seat, turning away from us, Sara blinks up at me.

"I guess I have a lot to fill you in on."

TWENTY-NINE

SARA

Dad's still at the office by the time I get home, which is ideal. I don't want him to know I'm going to Cute Neighbor Boy's apartment across the hall for tutoring, because then I'd have to explain my pretest grade. And also? He'd probably insist on introducing himself to Joe, and I'm just not mentally prepared for that yet.

One day, though. Hopefully when Joe's my official boyfriend.

A nervous flutter shifts in my belly. I'm going to Joe's place! Well, it's Oliver's place too. I'm choosing to ignore that, though.

I've tugged half of my short hair into a nubby ponytail, letting my bangs fall around my face. It's effortless in a casual way, I think, even though I *did* put effort in. I'm not going over in my uniform, though. That's just nerdy. But I'm also not going to dress like it's a big date or something. How embarrassing if I show up in a dress and he's in sweats!

I do, however, want to look pretty. Is that so wrong?

That's why I end up wearing my favorite jeans and salmon-pink hoodie, which fits me nicely. And, sure, I put a *tiny* bit of mascara on my lashes. Maybe I also swiped a *teeny* smudge of gloss over my lips. Sue me!

As I'm knocking on Joe's door across the hall, my heartbeat accelerates by the second. What if Oliver answers? Does he even know I'm coming over? Please, *please* don't let him answer the door. I can't bear an awkward interaction with him right now.

The door opens. "Sara, hi!"

I glance up. It's just Joe—*phew*.

Upon first assessment, I know I made the right wardrobe choice. Joe's wearing a cozy cotton tunic and navy joggers. You know, the type of thing one usually wears around the house. His hair flops over his forehead when he grins.

"It's so convenient you live right across the hall—come on in."

I step inside the threshold. "It's so nice in here. Thanks again for—"

My gaze ticks to my left, where I spot none other than Subwayboy sitting on the couch.

"Hey, Oliver, I invited Sara to study," Joe's saying. "We're going to work at the kitchen table."

Oliver's also not in his school uniform, because popular belief aside, he isn't a robot—I *suppose*. Jury may still be out. Similar to me, he wears a drawstring hoodie, only his is teal blue. But *un*like me and more like his brother, he has on dark joggers.

His eyes flick up from the book he's reading, and he glowers at me before focusing on Joe. "You want me to leave?"

"No, stay. We won't be loud, will we, Sara?"

"Um." I swallow. Dang it, why does he have to be here? "I mean, we'll probably be talking, right?"

Oliver closes his book. "I'll leave."

"Really, it's okay. We're just going to study," Joe insists.

"I do have a lot of questions, though. So I may talk a lot," I push, hoping Oliver continues to take this massive hint and leaves us alone.

"Oh, well, maybe we can whisper or something? But I don't want you to think you can't ask me anything. Huh, maybe we should—"

"Whatever, it's fine." Oliver collapses back on the couch. "I have earphones. Do whatever you want."

And then he pops his earbuds in and goes back to his book. I sneak a peek at the cover. Bruce Springsteen's memoir. Interesting. Oliver's always listening to music, so I guess that checks out. I would have bet all my money it was calculus related, but maybe this is why I'm so terrible with bets.

This brings me to my current problem. Oliver's staying. Here. In the room where Joe and I are gonna study. *Why?* What did I do to deserve this?

"Right! Let's get started, then."

Joe leads the way to the kitchen table, pulling out a chair and offering me a seat. So courteous.

As he settles in, I take an opportunity to look around. Two oak bookshelves line the walls behind the modular sofa Oliver sits on, his feet propped on a glass coffee table. It smells a little like leftover ramen and laundry detergent, an interesting combination.

The apartment is the same layout as ours, which isn't

surprising, but it's less decorated. The walls hold a few framed photographs of Joe and Oliver and someone who looks like their sister, but they're hung slightly crooked. I wonder if Joe put them up.

Their kitchen is like ours, an open-concept design that faces the living area, but while I decorated ours with embroidered tea towels, vanilla candles, and a pop of sky-blue paint, theirs is plain eggshell white with a stove that looks at least two decades old. Several baskets of snacks are organized on the countertop, though.

"Thanks again for your help, Joe," I say. "I was going to find a new tutor, but I appreciate you stepping in."

"Of course. Calculus can get really tough sometimes. We just have to keep trying, you know? If we focus tonight, we'll be prepared for the real test. And then we can relax and have fun at the school festival tomorrow."

"Totally," I agree, perking up. "I'm excited to work as a team on our first newspaper assignment."

Joe flips through his book. "You're bringing your cousin, right? Uh—" He peers over at me. "What's her name again?"

"Vicky? Yes, she's joining us."

What I don't say is that Vicky's agreed to hop on FaceTime to help me pick out the perfect outfit for this occasion, because if I'm going to get my first kiss from him, I want to look amazing.

"Right, Vicky! Great. Cool, um—okay!" He laughs, twirling his pencil between his fingers. "Let's do this, then."

My heart flutters as I pull out my homework. "I had a question about these problems here." I point. "I can't seem to get the right answer."

"Hmm, let me see."

Joe leans closer, and I track the smell of clean shampoo. How did I get so lucky? Just look at him. He's so perfect and nice. This moment would be ideal if Subwayboy wasn't on the couch behind me, ruining everything. He's probably watching me right now and hoping I fail.

Don't think about him, Sara.

"Yeah, these types of problems are pretty tough," he says after a moment. "Let me try—oh. Hang on."

I watch him work through the first couple of steps, then go back and erase all four lines.

"This is wrong." He tries again, now mumbling more to himself. "Is it like this? Wait—no. That's not right." He erases again. "Hey, Oliver, come here real quick. How do you solve this type of problem again?"

My eyes widen. *Noooooo*, my mind screams. Don't ask him! Joe, what are you *doing*? I loved that we were pretending Oliver wasn't here. Can we go back to that?

Oliver comes and stands beside me, picking up my homework and studying the problems. I tug on the strings of my pink hoodie, not daring to look at him. Ugh, so awkward.

"Okay. You're finding the derivatives of this function?"

"Yup," Joe confirms cheerily.

Oliver lowers himself into a crouched position and removes a pencil from his pocket, then works out the steps. "So, first you substitute—"

I don't hear anything else because I'm too focused on the way Oliver leans over his work, hair swooping over his forehead as he scrawls through the steps. We've never been this physically close. Not even in tutoring. His thick eyebrows furrow together when he's in the middle of solving, the tension dissolving in his forehead when things click in place.

Joe cups his chin in his palm as he studies Oliver's method. Is this really happening right now? I may as well be in tutoring with Oliver instead of Joe, seeing as he's the one helping us.

From beside him, Joe's phone lights up with an incoming call.

"Oh, it's Mom. One sec."

Then he stands, already walking toward the hall.

Nooooo! Don't leave me here with him!

"Hey, Mom, yeah—I know! Calm down, you're okay." Over his shoulder, Joe says, "Oliver, could you help her out for a minute? I won't be long."

His voice fades as he steps into his bedroom and closes the door behind him.

Oliver stares at me. I stare back.

Suddenly, I'm very warm.

Instead of crouching, he moves into the open chair beside me, sighing. Then he rolls his hoodie sleeves up to his elbows. What, are we about to do surgery or calculus?

"You don't have to help if you don't want—"

"Why?" He's already scribbling the final step in the problem. "You want to fail another test?"

I snap my eyes to his side profile. "What test? I didn't fail any—uh—"

Oliver raises his eyebrows, whistling a sweet, innocent tune as he casually spins his pencil toward me. As I take a closer look, I spot a familiar piggie sticker curved around the top.

A gasp lodges in my throat. Eyes widening, I jump to my feet, reaching out to snatch the pencil. "Hey! Where did you get that?"

Oliver raises his arm above his head before I have the chance to strike. "Found it on public property. Plus, it's stuck to my pencil. That means it's mine now."

I fall back in my chair, folding my arms across my chest. "Fine, *whatever.* You keep that. And, yes, I suck at calculus, but you already know that."

He points the eraser at me. "Okay, let's study, then."

Warily, I meet his eyes. "Really?"

"Yes, come on."

He sounds sincere. He's not even scowling or giving me a look like I chucked his backpack in the lake. Instead, he positions himself so he's a tad closer to me, so I unfold my arms and lean in.

"Okay." I pick up my pencil, braving a look at him. "Thanks, Oliver."

His eyes flick to mine before dropping to his work. "Yeah, no problem."

"Just don't yell at me."

"Who's yelling?" He taps the page with the eraser. "This section isn't that hard. I'll break it down—oh, look. Here's an easy one."

Huh, he's in a good mood today. No grouchiness in sight. Did I temporarily transport myself to a parallel universe where this Oliver is nice? Unlikely.

However, maybe this is my opportunity to tell him everything. No more secrets, no more lies. It's time to clear the air about the subway kiss bet. If I do, I'll have an easier time focusing. Really, it's for the benefit of my own mental health—and grade point average.

"So you multiply here—"

"Hold on, wait."

Oliver blinks at me. "You're already stuck? That was only step one."

Ouch. Definitely not a parallel universe.

"No, uh." I take a deep breath, uneasy. "I wanted to talk about something."

He studies me from behind his glasses, one brow arched. Then he leans back in his chair and crosses his arms.

How do I even begin?

"Uh, well. I—um."

He's staring at me, waiting for me to go on. I feel myself turning red. Surely he's noticed too.

"About the other night—*atthesubway*." The last part comes out in a rush, as if it's all one word.

Oliver glances down the hallway. "Uh, what night? I've never taken the subway."

But his neck is flushed, and now he won't meet my gaze. Sure, maybe he can see right through me, but I can *also* see right through whatever this act is. So I narrow my eyes, summon all my bravery, and take a deep breath.

"Cut it out, okay? I know you remember me."

Oliver drops his eyes to my homework. "Yeah, well. I guess it's hard to forget a random stranger coming up to you and asking to kiss you out of nowhere."

Then his eyes flick up to meet mine. Even though my

heart is rollicking inside my chest, I don't chicken out and look away. This is my moment. I'm not going to leave anything else unsaid.

"Okay, I get it. The whole situation was weird, but I have a perfectly reasonable explanation," I say. "You know my friend Patrick?"

"Unfortunately," he intones. "Were you trying to make him jealous or something?"

"What? No. Let me finish." I smooth my palms over my jeans. "Gosh, you're sure chatty tonight. Anyway—Patrick. Well, I've never—ugh. I can't believe I'm telling you this."

He waits, silent. What do I have to lose, really? He already called me a weirdo in the subway. What's he going to do now, say it again?

Okay, here goes nothing.

"I've never kissed anyone before, so Patrick dared me to go kiss you—a random stranger—so I could get it over with. And I know it was stupid to agree. Obviously, a first kiss should be special, right? But I wanted to prove I was, like, *brave*. Next thing I know, I'm suddenly marching up to you and asking—*agh*."

It's mortifying reliving this out loud, so I jump to the apology bit.

"I'm so sorry, Oliver. I shouldn't have, because now you think I'm a total weirdo. Which is fine. I guess."

Oliver places his forearms on the table and inches closer to me. "Okay, fine. Let's do this, then."

Uh, we're moving on from this topic that quickly? I mean, I should have assumed he wouldn't care *that* much, but I guess he really doesn't want to discuss this. Which is fair. Why would he? He's already moved on, and so have I.

I slip my pencil between my fingers. "Oh, studying. Right. Sorry."

"No," Oliver amends. "Your first kiss."

My head snaps up so fast I may have given myself whiplash.

What did he just say?

The corners of his mouth tilt up. "Come on, then."

"What?" I splutter, dizzy with confusion.

"You *just* said you wanted to get it over with, right?" He shifts forward in his chair, leaning in even farther.

And—oh my. His eyes are a kaleidoscope of greens. A lighter mossy color in some areas and a richer jade in others. Captivating, really.

Then it hits me.

Oliver Yang is about to *kiss me*.

Here.

At his kitchen table.

Do I want that?

"Ah, wait!" I slap my hands over my face. "No! I'm saying it was stupid of me to ask you that one time. I wasn't thinking, clearly. And I don't want it to happen like this—with all this math homework everywhere." I squeeze my eyes shut as I admit the rest. "I actually want my first kiss to feel special, you know? With someone I really like."

"Relax, Sara."

Huh?

I lower my hands. Oliver is still close, so close I can spot the lighter shades of golden blond mixing with darker strands as his hair shifts.

He grins. "I was kidding."

And then the little prankster starts laughing. *Laughing!*

My fingers connect with his chin, pushing his face away from mine.

"Why are you laughing at me?" I demand. "After I just told you all that? How embarrassing."

Oliver leans back in his chair, still smiling. He should really do that more often. Smile, I mean. Not try to kiss me.

"Hey, you did the same thing to me, remember? I had to re-create the moment. Consider it payback."

Then he winks. It happens so fast that I think I've imagined it. Wow, I haven't seen this side of him. Relaxed. Playful, even. Is Oliver Yang *fun*? Who knew?

My surprise must show on my face, because he laughs harder. It's not mean laughter, though, and dimples appear on either side of his cheeks as he grins. It's very adorable, which only causes my blush to deepen.

I thought he was cute the night I spotted him at the subway, but he's been so grumpy to me ever since. This Oliver is tolerable. If he'd acted like this from the start, maybe we'd be friends.

"Okay, I'm back!"

As Joe reenters the room, I fling back in my chair, putting space between myself and Oliver. If Joe thinks this is odd, he doesn't show it.

"Mom's just having another panic attack about the wedding," he goes on. "She keeps calling me every five minutes."

"Your mom is getting married?"

"Yeah, she left my dad a while ago and now she's remarrying for the third time," Joe explains. "It's kind of crazy, I know."

"Oh, I'm sorry." I shift my gaze to Oliver, who's suddenly gone stony again. "That must be hard."

"Nah, it's fine. It's just hard when we're all spread out like this." Joe looks between us. "I heard you guys laughing—what's so funny? Did you finally figure out that problem?"

Oliver covers his mouth to hide his smirk and, unfortunately, covers those dimples. I swallow my own chuckle. This whole situation is *sort of* funny. I mean, who would have thought I'd not only live across from the random boy I tried to kiss, but that he'd end up as my tutor? Oh, and that I have a big ole crush on his older brother?

"Nope," Oliver says simply, then rises to his feet. His eyes linger on mine, just for a moment, something softening behind them. But then he cuts away to address Joe. "It was way too difficult."

Joe scratches the back of his head. "Huh. Really?"

"Yes." Oliver's already moving down the hall. "Maybe you'll be able to figure it out—sorry."

I watch him leave. What the heck was that all about? Who would've known Subwayboy was such a little flirt?

But—wait. Does that mean he's going to tutor me again?

No! Geez. What am I thinking? I have Joe now.

Joe sits next to me, then picks up his pencil and studies Oliver's work. "Is it really that hard?"

"Everything about calculus is hard," I supply, which is unhelpful but honest.

"Let's see if I can manage."

If he can't, I have no idea what I'm going to do. I imagine knocking on Oliver's bedroom door, begging him to help me again, and shiver. No thank you. I won't lose any more of my dignity today.

On the bright side, I finally confessed to Oliver. It's all

out in the open. No more secrets. Who cares if he knew the entire time? It's in the past now. I don't have to stress about it anymore. And he took it surprisingly well. I mean, he got me back with his little joke, so now we're square.

Agh, but I told him I wanted my first kiss to feel special! Is that sappy? Does he assume I'm some pathetic hopeless romantic? Maybe Patrick's right. Boys don't think about romance the way girls do. Kisses aren't something they dream about. Oliver probably thinks I should just get it over with too.

"Oh! I finally figured it out." Joe tilts my homework so we can both read it. "So, this is how you do it—"

He begins patiently walking through each step in the problem, and by the time he reaches the end, I think I understand a little better than before. So he has me try the next one, and he's encouraging when I make a mistake, ensuring I go back and try again. Eventually, I figure it out.

"You're so smart, Joe. Thank goodness we have your brain here to help us."

Joe only grins.

I may have bombed the pretest, but the real test is tomorrow. With Joe's help, I'm going to do better. I *know* it. If I don't, I may as well kiss my dreams of going to the festival with him goodbye.

And I'm determined *not* to let that happen.

THIRTY

PATRICK

As soon as I get home from school I close my bedroom door and riffle through the love letters and gifts that tumbled from my locker. Some envelopes carry a sweet plum scent. Others are sealed with glittery heart stickers. Each letter is addressed to me, my name written in tidy handwriting that gives nothing away.

I'm wondering who could have written them when Sara Lin pops into my mind. I replay the way she threw her arms around me, burying her head in my chest as she apologized. We're not huggers. I mean, we've never been physically affectionate with each other. That's what caught me off guard. Because hugging was new. And she did it, probably, because she was so upset.

That's all it meant.

It doesn't mean all these love letters are from her.

That ship sailed a while ago, didn't it?

I'm clasping a purple box, and open it to find various

chocolate truffles inside. After popping one in my mouth, I realize it's mint chocolate. My favorite.

"Patrick! Dinner's ready."

I scramble to close the box just as Mom swings open my door, eyeing the letters scattered across my bed.

"Are those—? Love letters? From girls?"

The truffle box tips from my hands. Chocolate scatters across my quilted bedspread.

"Mom! Can't you knock?"

"I can't believe this," she says, brushing aside chocolate and sitting next to me on the bed. She picks up a letter and starts reading: "'I can't stop staring at those ocean eyes. Love, your secret admirer.' Oh! Someone's in love with my beautiful son!"

I don't think there's anything worse than your own mother reading romantic letters addressed to you out loud.

"They're right. You do have such beautiful ocean eyes!"

"Mooom," I moan. "Stop."

"Sandy, what's going on in here?" Dad says as he barges into the room, eyeing us. "Leave our son alone. Don't you see he's busy with—?"

"Look, Bob!" Mom waves a letter in the air. "Our son has a secret admirer."

This is *such* an invasion of privacy. Why didn't I lock my door?

Dad sits on my other side and slides an arm around my shoulders. "Really, son? *Wow*. I'm so proud."

Ugh, this is the last thing I wanted.

"What's going on in here?"

Now Pearl's skipping into my room, and I want to melt into the floor and disappear from this realm.

"Your big brother's got a secret admirer," Mom says, fanning a handful of letters in front of her face so my little sister can see.

"Ooooo," Pearl coos, plucking one from her hand. "Are these from Sara Lin?"

"Oh! Patrick, *are* they from Sara?" Mom adds, acting way too nosy.

Before I can reply, my dad thumps a sturdy hand across my chest. "Son, when a man finally decides to love a woman—"

But he's cut off by Pearl screeching, "It's mint chocolate!" She's collected a few truffles in her hands and is already popping another into her mouth. "Patrick's favorite!"

"I always thought you two were made for each other," Mom tells me.

Pearl tosses a chocolate at my head. "How long have you been dating?"

"What are you all *talking* about?" I burst, face reddening. "Of course they're not from Sara Lin!"

Mom blinks. "Are you sure?"

"Yes, I'm sure. *Please* just leave me alone. I can't deal with you all barging in on my life like this." I scoop letters into my backpack then sling it over my shoulders. "I'm outta here."

And that's how I end up at Kiki's Chicken Kitchen. Vicky's a reasonable person of sound mind, unlike my family, and she'll know what to do.

We find an empty table in the back corner. She makes sure her manager can't see us before she turns to me, arms folded over her apron.

"You've got five minutes."

I dump the contents of my bag on the table.

Vicky watches a candied heart roll off the surface and onto the floor. "Uh, thanks?"

"No—what? These aren't for you," I amend, reaching down to grab the rogue candy. "I found them in my locker, and I need your help figuring out who they're from."

"What are you coming to me for? I don't even go to your school. How am I supposed to know who has a crush on you?"

"Because, well, I don't know, exactly." I stumble over my words. "But you're smart. Help me figure this out."

She just stares at me, long and hard, and then says, "You think they're from Sara, don't you?"

Heat rushes into my cheeks. "What? Um, I hadn't considered that."

A lie. A big, giant, stinkin' lie. Vicky's eyes narrow like she doesn't believe me.

"Do *you* think they might be from Sara?" I ask in what I hope is a casual tone.

"No, but good luck finding out. I gotta get back to work."

She's on her feet, long hair swishing over her shoulders as she heads to the kitchen. But I can't let her leave. Not yet.

I step in front of her, blocking her path.

"Wait! Why'd you say no like that? They could totally be from Sara, right? She likes writing poems and stuff, and she knows my favorite candy *and* my locker combination. And aren't you forgetting she used to have a crush on me?"

Vicky remains unenthused. "Listen, I don't know who they're from, but they're definitely not from Sara. All she talks about is her new crush, Joe."

My eyes widen, but I should have expected this. Before our fight, Joe was all Sara wanted to talk about.

"I even tried asking her about you and she just changed the subject," Vicky continues. "If you really want Sara to send you love letters or something, I suggest you start working for it. Do something about it. Because, to me, it sounds like she's quickly moving on."

There's this uncomfortable twitch in my gut. Moving on? It sounds so dramatic. But haven't I seen it with my own eyes? Sara eating lunch with Joe. Walking to school with Joe. *Texting* Joe. Argh, she's even in Newspaper Club with him!

It's one thing to suspect it myself, but it's another thing to hear this from Vicky, who arguably knows Sara best.

Three bowls arrive in the kitchen window, and the cook motions for Vicky to run them to the appropriate table. She heads that way, but not before telling me, "Let me know whenever you figure it out."

So that's it. Sara's moving on. Unless I do something about it, I'm going to lose her to Joe.

And I *can't* lose.

THIRTY-ONE

SARA

"Dad! Are you kidding me?"

I'm scrambling around the kitchen like a cricket that's accidentally been let loose indoors. I grab my blazer slung on the back of a kitchen chair, then hop two inches left and dive for my shoulder bag. Did I remember to put on deodorant? I sniff and—yes. All good. Dad just watches me from his seat at the table.

"Why didn't you wake me up earlier?" I go on. "I'm gonna be late for my test!"

Dad sets his coffee down. "You're a grown adult, Sara. You should be waking *me* up."

I pause in the middle of tying my shoe. How does that even make any sense?

"Oh, so *now* I'm a grown adult? But the other night when *I* wanted—"

"You're late!" Dad interrupts, skirting around my argument. "Hurry up!"

I came home from studying at Joe's before Dad arrived home from the office. This was an intentional move on my part. Dad trusts Mr. Yang—we've been neighbors for years—but he does not know that Mr. Yang's two sons now live with him. If he did know, I'm sure I'd get a lecture faster than you can say *inverse hyperbolic functions.*

Oh yes, that's right. I retained some calculus last night. I even stayed up late reviewing on my own in my bedroom. How's that for priorities, Subwayboy?

I shrug my bag around my shoulder, about to slip out the door, when my dad says, "And don't forget, if you don't pass your test, you can't go to the school festival tonight." He raises his coffee to his lips. "And no TV for a month."

Wow, as if I didn't know this already. Good thing he has no idea I failed yesterday's pretest.

"Gee, great words of encouragement, Dad. Thank you."

"Have an amazing *daaaaay*!" he singsongs as I leave.

No pressure. I simply have to pass a real calculus test or forgo attending the festival with Joe and Vicky, which is all I've been looking forward to since I joined Newspaper Club.

As I tug the door closed, I hear shuffling from behind me. I look over my shoulder and find Oliver locking his apartment, a granola bar clenched between his teeth.

"Good morning," I blurt, suddenly frazzled in his presence.

"Uh," he starts, removing the granola bar. "Morning!"

Huh. Polite interaction achieved. Who knew?

Maybe coming clean yesterday did help.

And then I remember—oh crap. The calculus test!

I race to the elevator. "I'm running kind of late," I say as I smash the Down button.

Oliver saunters over, peering over my shoulder. Why is this the morning the elevator is slower than usual? I keep jamming the button with my palm, as if *this* will speed up its arrival.

It doesn't. Lucky me.

Then I realize Oliver is alone.

I toss a glance his way. "Is Joe coming?"

"Nope, he's already at school." He raises his eyebrows. "Because you have that test first period."

With a melodic *ping*, the doors open. Hallelujah! Finally!

"Yeah, I'm aware—that's why I just said I'm running late—but thanks for the reminder."

Once we step inside, I hit the Lobby button approximately twenty thousand times. Then, because I am tortured by modern technology, the doors take their sweet time sliding closed.

"You know," Oliver begins lazily, "that won't make it go any faster."

I jerk my hand away from the button. "Right."

With a low groan, the elevator starts its descent. I tap my foot anxiously, hoping it won't stop for anyone else so we can get down faster. Oliver eats his granola bar, and I rack my brain for something to say so the silence isn't awkward.

"So, the festival is tonight," I say, angling my head so I'm looking at him. "That'll be fun. You know, because of newspaper and everything."

Oliver swallows a bite, then says, "Ah, well, only if you pass your test—right?"

"Yes, right." I swing my shoulder bag off my shoulders and let it thump to the floor, then tug my arms through my blazer. "I know that."

"So, was Joe a better tutor for you, then?"

I've crouched to pick up my bag, and am rising to my full height as our gazes lock. He's wearing an expression so neutral you might as well call it taupe. He's not a closed book; he's a safe that's welded shut. How am I supposed to answer that?

"Joe? Yeah—he's great! So smart and all," I say, and then find that I cannot. Stop. Talking. "Incredible, really. But, um, you already know that."

A nervous laugh burbles from my lips. Oliver gives me sidelong stare that's equally unperturbed and cool. Is it weird that I miss his laugh? Because I do.

"I guess we'll see how it goes after I take this te—"

Clang!

A rumbling under our feet causes us to sway into each other. Our shoulders bump. When we restabilize, my eyes jump to his just as the lights flicker.

The elevator does not move.

The doors do not open.

And, most importantly, I do not panic.

But Oliver does.

"Wha—what was that?" His hand leaps to his chest, and his voice sounds airy and flustered. "What's with the lights? Why did we stop?"

I jam the Lobby button again. "Oh, don't worry. This elevator is old. It does weird stuff all the time."

Oliver pales. "Weird stuff?"

Huh, usually that works. Now, I punch a series of buttons, tapping them in curt repetition. Come on, elevator. Not today. I can't miss this test!

"It's not working because you keep doing *that*," Oliver snaps, gesturing to the control panel. "Stop!"

"You've got to trust me." I move my finger from the Lobby button to the Door Open button. "I've gotten stuck in here a bunch of times before—"

"*Stuck?*" Oliver's back hits the wall and his arms are spread wide, one hand still grasped around his granola bar. "No, *please* don't tell me we're stuck."

Perspiration beads along his temples. His chest rises and falls in rapid succession. I've never seen him this nervous.

I turn back to the panel. If I press the Emergency button, it's gonna take service forever to get here, and then I'll for sure miss my test. I know I can fix this. I just have to keep Oliver calm while I do.

"There's nothing to worry about," I reassure him. "Are you claustrophobic?"

Instead of answering, he gives me a terrified look.

Okay, so that's a yes.

"Just pretend you're at the beach and leave the rest to me—I know some good tricks. You have to keep pressing this combination." I use the heel of my shoe for extra pressure, then shift to my other foot to give the button a swift kick. "Like this."

The elevator jounces. With a heavy lurch, we continue our final descent and, a second later, the doors open. Freedom!

"See?" I spin toward Oliver. "All good!"

Oliver's still backed into the corner, frozen in timid panic. Perhaps he needs a minute.

I leap from the threshold, exiting. "All right, well, gotta run! Wish me luck on my test!"

There's no time to wait around for his reply, so I rush toward the double doors. But just as I'm approaching them, I hear him call, "Good luck, Sara Lin!"

Pivoting around, I find him standing on the other side of the elevator doors, which are rattling closed behind him. His tousled golden hair flops across his forehead as he tips his chin, a hint of a smile gracing his lips. Shy, but it's there. Oliver believes in me!

"Yes! Time to pass this stupid test!" I holler, my voice echoing through in the empty lobby.

Who cares if I'm loud? I'm about to seize these numbers by the ankles and shake them until the correct answer appears on the page.

And with this newfound determination, I sprint out of the building.

I *swear* I hear Oliver laughing as I dart away.

THIRTY-TWO

PATRICK

Look, I'm not trying to be nosy. It's just that Sara sits in front of me, and she's not exactly keeping her voice down.

We've just returned from lunch, and Mr. Day passed back our tests as we entered the classroom. I came to my seat as Sara waited for Mr. Day to find her test. Once it was in her hands, of course she went straight to Joe.

"Can you *believe* this?"

Joe's gaze drops to her test, and then his brows pinch together. "Oh? Wow, uh. Look at that!"

"Thank you *so much*," she gushes. "I can't believe I passed!"

I can't take it anymore, so I lean forward and squint, zeroing in on her paper. There's a giant 68% marked on top.

"That's great, really—but, uh, are you sure that's passing?" Joe asks.

"Unfortunately, I'm all too familiar with lower grades. Don't worry, it's passing." Her mouth breaks into a grin that reaches her eyes. "I couldn't have done it without you!"

And then I'm forced to watch as she throws her arms around him, squeezing his midsection.

Something uncomfortable twinges in my gut. I remember how she'd thrown her arms around me yesterday, her peach shampoo enveloping me as she buried her face into my chest. Now Joe knows how that feels.

Why do I suddenly hate that he's the one getting a hug right now?

I shift my gaze away from them, but not before I catch him saying, "Congratulations, Sara. I'm so proud of you."

It grates my last nerve. I snatch my water bottle from my desk and take my mopey self into the hallway, stopping at the water fountain. Sure I'm using this as an excuse to get away from their little display in there, but ugh. Spare me with the flirting.

Sara normally comes to me with her good news first. Since when does Joe get that privilege?

I refill my bottle. Vicky told me to do something about Sara, but what am I *supposed* to do? How can I do something when I'm not even sure how I feel about her yet?

A tinkling voice interrupts my thoughts. "I saw you glaring at those two without bothering to intervene. Is there something you're waiting for?"

When I turn around, I find Rose standing just beyond the classroom door, arms crossed. An unpleasant frown is splayed across her face, like she's just licked asphalt.

I don't like where this is going, so I resort to humor to save me.

"So you're saying you've been watching me?" I ask, wag-gling my brows. "Checking me out, are you, Rose?"

It works. She's immediately flustered. "No, that's not—"

"Come on. You *must* find me attractive if you can't stop staring at me." I leave my water bottle perched on the fountain and flex a biceps, planting a kiss on my smooth skin. "You can't tell me you haven't noticed these bad boys before."

"Please stop. I'm begging." Rose sighs and adjusts her headband—as if it needed adjusting; it's always perfectly in place. "I want to talk to you about something. It's about Joe and Sara. I think we should be helping each other."

My arms fall to my sides. What is she on about? Since when does Rose want anything to do with me, let alone want to help me?

But I'm curious.

"What do you mean?"

"I've noticed how your little friend Sara's been clinging to Joe lately, and obviously Joe's nice to everybody, so he's just going along with it," she explains, excitement building behind her eyes. "I'm sure he's not trying to lead her on, but I can see things ending in disaster if it continues like this. And I'm not gonna sit here and pretend I really care about Sara's well-being, but I know that you do. You don't want her to get hurt, right?"

I fold my arms over my chest, annoyed. Rose thinks she's *so* superior, but she doesn't know everything. Joe seems into Sara, which is why I'm in this predicament. Because, yes, maybe a teeny part of me wanted those love letters to be from Sara.

But is it because I miss her attention? Or is it because I really like her?

As more than a friend?

"So what are you saying?" I snap. "Get to the point."

"That's why I said we should help each other." Rose moves her hands onto her hips. "Joe and I obviously have our thing going on, and everyone knows we're the better match. And even though you might try and deny it, I know you have a thing for Sara. You can't stop staring at her. I saw you in there just now. And she's obviously always had a thing for you, Patrick. Everyone knows that."

I press my lips together. This used to irritate me to no end. (Can't a guy and a girl be friends? Sheesh.) But now . . . I don't know. It doesn't bother me as much, I guess.

"Joe is getting in the way, and I can see how it complicates things between you two," she continues. "So what do you say? We can help each other, don't you see?"

My, isn't Rose so perceptive? Although Sara wasn't exactly being subtle when she threw her arms around Joe just now. And don't I want Joe out of the equation?

Ugh, bad calculus pun.

"So," I say slowly, "are you saying you wanna split them up?"

She chuckles, placing a hand lightly on my shoulder. "Oh Patrick, *split them up*? I wouldn't call it that—they're not even dating. But more like . . . prevent Sara Lin from experiencing heartbreak." She leans closer to my ear. "You care about Sara, right? If you do, we could do this together."

I do care about Sara, but she's her own person. Her feelings aren't mine to complicate, and I'm definitely not going to team up with I Get What I Want Rose to demolish any chance Sara might have with Joe. I'm not about to be used by the popular girl *and* ruin my best friendship.

So I shove Rose's hand from my shoulder, putting distance

between us. "Ha, you're funny," I intone. "Sounds like you want to use me, but guess what? Me and Sara are just friends, so who am I to stop her from dating whoever she wants?"

Rose huffs, offended. I pluck my water bottle from the fountain and tuck it under my arm, starting for the classroom.

"Sorry, I'mma pass this time," I say coolly. "Looks like you're gonna have to woo Joe the old-fashioned way. You're really pretty, though, so I'm sure you'll have no trouble."

"What, Patrick? Did you even hear a word I said?" She catches up to me quickly. "This isn't just about me—it's a win-win situation! I'd be using you as much as you'd be using me. That's why I said we're helping each other."

I wave a hand through the air, as if dismissing her. "Still no, but thanks for the consideration. I'm honored you thought of me for your evil plan. Maybe next time."

"Whatever, Patrick," she huffs, blowing several light strands of hair out of her face. "Don't mind me saying *I told you so* after Sara comes crying to you because Joe's broken her weak little heart, especially when you could have been there to prevent it in the first place."

I've come *this* close to escaping Rose, but this makes me pause in the doorway. I weigh her words. What if Rose is right? Joe's nice to everyone. Maybe he's actually into Rose but Sara can't tell. If that's true, Sara's gonna be devastated. I imagine her giving up writing forever, too depressed to write or hang out or eat hot pot—

I shudder. No, I can't let that happen.

Rose must sense a shift in me, because she says, "If you're not doing this for me, at least do it for her. You care about her well-being even just as friends, right?"

I turn and face her, taking cautious steps forward. "Okay, I'm just asking questions here, but what would we even do about it, Rose? It's not like I'm just gonna go up to her and—"

A mischievous glint appears behind her eyes as she smirks. "Just come with me, I'll take care of everything." Then she struts ahead of me, making a beeline for the classroom. "I even have a plan for tonight, and all you have to do is show up to the festival."

Whoa, whoa, whoa! I gave an inch and she took a mile. There's no way I'm teaming up with freaking Rose. No. Way.

I catch up to her. "What? Hey, stop. I didn't agree to anything!"

"Just follow my lead, Patrick."

And then she practically skips inside Mr. Day's room, humming gleefully under her breath. Oh no—what in the world is she going to do?

"Wait," I say, chasing after her. "I *just* said I didn't even agree to anything!"

THIRTY-THREE
SARA

I've drawn my attention away from Joe, ready to twirl over to Patrick's desk and show him my grade, when I notice he's not at his desk. Huh. He got his test before I did, though we still have a few more minutes until the bell rings. I guess he stepped out.

"I just wish I would've been a better tutor last night," Joe's saying. "As much as I understand some math, it's not my strongest subject."

Agh, he's so kind! And so hard on himself, which I don't want. I wouldn't have passed without his guidance. Oliver tried, too, I guess. So did Vicky.

Geez, it really does take a village.

He runs his fingers through his hair, his elbows resting on the flat surface of my desk, and a tiny thrill zings through my chest when his eyes meet mine.

"Don't worry, you helped me so much," I say. "And now I can go to the festival tonight, so really, *thank you.*"

"But we have to get your grades higher so you can stay in Newspaper Club, right?"

Oh. Right. That's true.

"You told me writing was something you love," he continues. "So if you want to spend more time doing it, I say we figure out a way to help you. Maybe it's best if you got an official tutor."

Uh, hold on. Is he not my official tutor now?

"A tutor?" I say weakly.

"Yeah! A real tutor will be perfect—oh! I got it!" He snaps his fingers, eyes lighting up. "My little brother, Oliver."

You. Have. Got. To. Be. Kidding. Me.

"He's a math tutor—why didn't I think of this before? And he's looking for more students. He's trying to save money to buy a guitar."

Joe means well, which is why I am not about to tell him his brother used to tutor me. And that he sort of *did* tutor me while Joe was on the phone with their mom last night.

Does this mean Joe doesn't want to spend time together? Or is he really trying to look out for my best interests?

"But I thought you—" I stop short, just now processing the last thing he said about Oliver. "A guitar?"

He pulls out his phone from his pocket. "Yeah! He's really good. Let me text you his number. This is perfect! I don't know why I didn't think of this, uh—"

I must have a dejected look on my face, because he reaches out and nudges my chin up with his index finger. My heart flutters at his contact.

"Don't worry, okay? We'll figure this out," Joe says gently, dropping his hand. "He's gonna help you get your grades up,

I promise. He's really smart. I know school can be stressful, and sometimes it's hard to believe we can accomplish difficult things, but you are amazing, Sara Lin! And smart. You can do this."

All my thoughts have zeroed in on the spot where he lightly touched my chin. Now he's smiling at me like I'm the only one in the room and—

"What's this?"

Before I can stop her, Rose swipes my test and holds it in front of her eyes, scanning my grade.

"Not the best mark, huh? But at least you passed."

Why does everyone keep saying that? Sixty-eight percent is a C minus, for Pete's sake. Sure, I'm not a genius, but that's passing!

Patrick rushes over a second later, almost like he's been chasing her. But that doesn't make any sense. Still, his lips slip into an aggravated frown as he tries to subtly nudge her in the ribs.

What's going on?

"Anyway," Rose continues, swatting him away like he's a gnat. "That means you'll be joining us at the festival later, I presume? Which is good, because we'll need all the help we can get." She flashes a smile at Joe. "Oh, and Joe? I have some things I wanted to run by you for the festival tonight. Do you mind?" She gestures to her desk, then cuts her eyes to me. "Besides, Patrick just told me he wants some alone time with Sara."

"What?" Patrick blurts.

Rose whacks him in the stomach with the hand that's still holding my test. He grunts as he takes it from her, but he won't meet my eyes.

"You know, to talk about some *private things* he's been wanting to tell her."

Patrick glares at her, but Rose doesn't notice because her attention is latched on Joe.

Private things? What the heck is she talking about?

Joe, in his overeager fashion, rises from his seat. "Okay, sure," he says, then trails behind Rose as they walk to her desk.

"Good luck!" Rose tosses from over her shoulder, blond hair swishing as she leaves us to it. Whatever "it" is.

I snap my gaze up at Patrick. "Private things? What's she talking about?"

"Uh, she's just kidding around." He stares down at my test. "Oh, wow. Look at this! You did, uh, great!"

I snatch the paper from his grip as he comes around to sit in Joe's empty desk. "It's not *great*, but at least I passed."

"Yeah, it's pretty terrible, I guess."

He seems nervous. It's in the way he's tapping his fingers over the desk, eyes darting to the window, back to Rose, and then over to me. There's never been a time in our friendship when Patrick had trouble telling me about anything, so what's freaking him out right now?

"Tell me what's going on," I say, searching his eyes for some sort of clue. "Are you okay? Should I be worried?"

"Uh," he says, which isn't an answer at all.

And then he leans closer, scrutinizing me.

"What?" I demand.

"Are you wearing makeup?"

He reaches out like he's going to poke my cheek, but I smack his hand away. "Don't ruin it!"

"Since when do you wear makeup?"

"Since when do you care?" I fire back, annoyed he's avoiding all my questions. "What's Rose's deal? What did she say you wanted?"

"Geez, Sara Lin. So moody. I was just trying to compliment you."

I sigh, crossing my arms. "No, you were just about to make fun of me. Now tell me what's going on." I fling my arm toward Rose. "You just made her steal Joe away from me right as we were having a *moment*."

He narrows his eyes, but I glare right back. I can do this all day.

"Never mind," he grumbles, getting up. "I'm going to the bathroom."

"Wait—"

But he doesn't. He weaves through desks and snatches the hall pass Mr. Day keeps near his chalkboard before racing from the classroom. Whatever "private thing" he needed to discuss with me must not matter much, but it's frustrating because Rose seems to know what it is. Meanwhile, I'm clueless.

"That was kind of harsh, Sara Lin."

I turn to the seat next to me and find Tammy fiddling with the end of one of her braided pigtails.

"You don't even know what he was gonna say," she continues.

Oh geez, was she eavesdropping? Not that I care. I mean, Patrick didn't reveal anything of importance, anyway.

"But—" I drop my head in my hands. "Ugh, you're right. Why do I keep snapping at him? He was just teasing. Classic Patrick."

"Patrick does tease a lot." Tammy cups her chin in her

palm, and this dreamy look falls over her. "You're so lucky. I wish he'd tease me like that."

"What? Why?"

"Oh, um, look! Mr. Day!"

Glancing at the door, I see that Mr. Day is, in fact, heading into the classroom. But when I glance at Tammy sidelong again, the apples of her cheeks turn pink. She nervously flips through her textbook, avoiding my gaze.

"Better get focused, right?"

"Right," I agree, pressing back a smile.

Well, well, well. Maybe I'm jumping to conclusions, but . . . is Tammy into Patrick?

I suppose I'll have to find out for myself.

THIRTY-FOUR

PATRICK

Thankfully, gym is our last period of the day, because the last thing I want to do is sit in my own sweat through several more classes. Honestly, I don't know anyone who wants to do that, especially when Coach Garcia makes us run the mile.

Which she's decided we're doing.

I don't mind running, but today I've slowed to a jog because it's chilly and I'm already hungry. Tammy's keeping a decent pace as she sticks to my side. Ever since we spent all those lunch periods together when I was in a fight with Sara, Tammy's been way more talkative. I've learned all about her favorite mochi donut spot, that she likes reading only fantasy books, and that she's saving up to see her favorite K-pop group when they come to town in a few months. She's easy to talk to, but it doesn't mean I didn't miss Sara when we weren't speaking.

Right now, I'm glad Tammy's not trying to make too much conversation, focused as she is on controlling her breath as she runs alongside me. Because honestly? I've been in my head about Rose's proposal.

On the one hand, I want to protect Sara from heartbreak, especially if Joe isn't interested in her. Even if he *is* interested in her, Rose will make sure she's the one who gets him in the end. Whenever she wants something, she goes after it and doesn't back down.

I wouldn't be a good friend if I didn't try to protect Sara, right?

But—ugh! I don't want to get involved in Sara's business, and this definitely falls into the meddling category. She's an adult, isn't she? Shouldn't I let her lead her own life?

"Beep, beep!"

Sara Lin pulls up on my left, hiking her knees to her chest as she runs. "Move it, slowpoke. The King of England could run faster than you."

I suppress an eye roll. "I'm tired, it's cold, it's windy, and I'm hungry."

"It *is* pretty chilly out." Tammy rubs her hands together. "Besides, he already did two laps. Didn't you see him? He's really fast."

Sara doesn't respond, because her attention lingers on the loud conversation happening behind us.

"Joe is so hot! Look at him run. Oh my gosh."

"Bet he has a six-pack."

"Totally. You can see it every time his shirt bounces when he runs."

I tense, irritation crawling up my spine. Sara blinks her focus back to me, trying to pretend she wasn't listening. Too late. We all heard.

"Uh, what were you going to tell me earlier?" she asks.

"Oh, uh—"

How do I warn her about Rose without sounding like I'm involved? Do I say, *Hey, Sara, Rose wants Joe to be her boyfriend so she's going to sabotage whatever's going on between you. By the way, what* is *going on between you?*

If there was anything to share, Sara would have told me. Wouldn't she? Why am I so obsessed with the thought of them spending time with each other? I have no trouble sharing Sara's friendship with Tammy when we get together, but the thought of hanging out with her and Joe drives me bonkers. My jaw gets tense and tight, and this weird emotion stirs frustration and neediness in my stomach.

I'm not jealous, am I? I mean, I really don't want Sara to get hurt by Rose, but is that all there is to it?

The chatter behind us increases in volume.

"He's *sooo* fast. I bet he could outrun all the guys!"

Sara clears her throat. "So, are you gonna tell me or—?"

"I wish he was my boyfriend!"

"All the guys in our class suck compared to him, so lame and boring."

As if on cue, Joe swoops past us with a polite "Hey, Sara!" Then he tosses her a wink before carrying on running.

Sara visibly swoons, and that right there is my final straw. My blood boils. A surge of adrenaline pulses through my veins. Do all these girls really think us guys are losers compared to Joe? Well, time to show them. He won't look like such a *hotshot* if I'm faster than him.

So I bolt away from Sara and Tammy in an attempt to pass him.

I concentrate on my breathing, really pushing my legs to the max, as I pick up speed. And with this extra concentrated effort, I'm suddenly zooming past Joe.

Ha! Take that, new guy.

But then Joe quickly catches up, keeping an intense pace with me. I use all the fuel in my tank to speed up, telling myself I'm not getting winded, that I can make another push and come out ahead.

We curve around the track field, still neck and neck, then our coach hollers, "Boys, this is just a warm-up! Why are you racing?"

But then I hear the girls chanting. "Go Joe! *Go Joe!*"

Of course they want Joe to win. This only makes me run faster.

When we clear the next curve, Joe drops behind me. Ha! Who's the hotshot now? I spare a glance over my shoulder and find him with both hands on his thighs, kneeling over to catch his breath, sweat trickling from his hairline and running down his cheeks.

I throw my hands in the air. I did it—I beat him!

However, my victory is fleeting. As soon as I rotate to face forward, my center of gravity fails me. It happens in an instant, so quickly that I don't have time to right myself. My shoe catches on the ground, and I'm flying through the air before crashing onto the track.

Right on my arm.

THIRTY-FIVE

SARA

"Ah! That freaking *hurts.*"

After watching Patrick all but face-plant onto the track, Tammy, Joe, and I volunteered to take him directly to the school nurse. Now we're clustered around him as he sits on the recovery couch while Nurse Kelly wraps his wrist in a bandage.

"Please hold still," the nurse says through a sigh.

I reach for Patrick's good hand and squeeze. "You're okay, Patrick."

From beside me, Tammy's gaze drops to our intertwined hands. I couldn't help but notice that the entire time Patrick was racing Joe, she was cheering for *Patrick*. And when I'd turned to look at her, a flush crept into her cheeks. Between her comment in the classroom and wanting Patrick to win the nonrace that turned into a race, I wonder if she's starting to like him as more than a friend. The blush was a familiar reaction; the same one I get whenever I'm around Joe.

"Do you think it's broken?" Joe asks the nurse.

"Hmm, maybe." She pins the wrap in place. "But I'm no doctor. Best thing you can do is get to the hospital for some X-rays, so I've called your parents. They're going to pick you up and take you."

"Great. I'm sure Mom is thrilled." Patrick groans.

Nurse Kelly checks her watch, then starts for the door. "School's just about over. You're all free to go—unless you want to wait here with Patrick."

Once she leaves us in the nurse's station, Joe turns to Patrick. He's suddenly bashful, hand lingering on the back of his neck.

"I'm so sorry about this, Patrick. I feel partly responsible," he says. "I hope it's nothing serious. Please let me know if there's anything I can do to help."

Patrick's eyes jump to his. "Actually, there's one thing. It's really important."

My brows furrow as I glance between them.

"What is it?" Joe asks.

"Declare I'm the fastest runner." Patrick smirks, his mischievous side returning even though he still looks a little pale. "Wasn't it a competition? And don't sweat my fall, dude. That was my fault."

"Oh! Okay! Yeah, you really did beat me, Patrick." Joe barks out a good-natured laugh. "I've got to run—and Sara? I'll see you at the festival tonight, right?"

As he asks this, he lays a hand on my shoulder.

Eee! First he touches my chin, now my shoulder? I don't want to read into this too much, but is it possible he likes me back? And if he does, could it mean Joe might be my first kiss?

"Right," I say, head spinning in the best way.

His smile widens. "You worked really hard for it. Let's make sure we have fun."

It feels as though my bones have transformed into maple syrup, because I'm melting into a puddle of goo before his radiant gaze.

He walks backward toward the door. "Take care, Patrick!" he says before he heads out, footsteps fading down the hall.

"Bye!" I shout, hoping he can still hear me, then spin on the heel of my foot to Patrick.

"Ahh, did you see that? He totally likes me, right?" I slide both hands over my cheeks, feeling the warmth growing there. "I have to go home and get ready!"

"You're leaving?" Patrick blurts, panic building behind his eyes. "What if I trip and break my other arm?"

I giggle, because I assume he's joking. He's known for that, after all.

"Don't be silly, that won't happen."

"But what if it does!" he insists, his tone serious now. "What if I break my legs too?"

"You're being ridiculous. Besides, Tammy is here." I sweep my arm toward her. "You'll stay with him, right, Tammy?"

I wouldn't call myself high maintenance, but I *did* just finish running a mile in gym, so I absolutely need a shower. Plus, I've got to have time to do my hair and makeup. Everything needs to be perfect for tonight. I won't settle for less.

Tammy's staring at Patrick's bandaged wrist. Suddenly, she throws her arms around his neck. "You have such great arms and legs, Patrick! And amazing ocean-colored eyes—I can't stop thinking about them—"

And then, as if realizing what's she's done, she launches off him and rushes to the door, clasping a hand over her mouth. "I'm sorry. That was—I mean—I—"

Without another word, she sprints out of the nurse's office.

My eyes connect with Patrick's, and he runs his good hand through his hair, brows pinched together. "That was kind of weird, right?"

A laugh escapes my lips. Oh my gosh, this all makes sense now!

"I'm pretty sure she has a crush on you," I tell him.

"Huh." He processes this information, and I can't tell if he's excited by this or not. Do I want that? For him to be excited? "Guess I found out who wrote me all those love letters, then."

I tilt my head, my heart constricting at this news. "Love letters? What love letters?"

"Oh. Um. I found some anonymous love letters in my locker." He gazes up at me through his eyelashes. "At first I thought they might have been from you, but that wouldn't have made any sense, would it?"

"Why didn't you tell me?" I force out a laugh, even though I'm not sure how I feel about this. Am I okay with Tammy liking Patrick? What if he likes her back? "And don't worry, I won't write you any more bad poetry. That ship sailed long ago—and it left without you!"

I'm hoping this will make him feel better, but Patrick casts his eyes to the floor. "Oh."

Okay. Something's up.

I sit next to him on the recovery couch. "Hey, what's wrong?"

"Hm?"

"Do you—" I blink, fingers toying with the hem of my gym shirt. "Do you wish I'd been the one to write you those love letters?" I nudge his biceps with my elbow. "What, don't tell me you're falling for me now?"

He winces. "Ouch—my arm!"

"Oh, oops. Sorry!" I hadn't realized I'd nudged the bandaged arm. "You okay?"

"Yeah."

"Okay, good."

We fall silent. Patrick stares at his gym shorts, and I stare at Patrick staring at his gym shorts. I don't know what else to say, but I've got to say *something*.

"Sara—" he starts just as I go, "I was—"

We stop. Look at each other.

"You go," he insists.

"Oh, well," I begin, hoping the right words come to me. "I was kidding with that comment. When I told you I liked you back then? I mean, things were awkward for a second, and I don't want that to happen again. But you've been acting kind of strange lately, so I was thinking—I don't know—maybe?"

Patrick's cheeks flush. "Listen, Sara. I just think—how do I say this?" He lets out a breath. "I haven't really thought about what I wanted to say to you."

I swallow. Wait, does Patrick like me now? Or does he want to tell me he's into Tammy, and would it be weird if he starts hanging out with her more?

How *would* I feel about that?

For so long, all I wanted was for Patrick to like me as more than a friend. We'd built this dynamic friendship, supporting each other through hard times and joking with each other during lighter ones. He knows everything about me, and I'm willing to bet I know everything about him. That's a bet I'm confident I'd win.

All romance movies ever taught me is that the guy always ends up falling for the girl in the end. Is this the moment I've hoped for? Where he tells me he has feelings for me?

"Your new crush on Joe is great and cool and whatever, honestly." He goes on, "I'm glad you found someone you really like. But, uh. I don't know. I'm sorry I've been a jerk lately. I guess I'm afraid I'll get replaced by whoever your new boyfriend might be." He holds my gaze. "Sara, you're my best friend. I'd be so sad to lose you. Yeah . . . so. That's all I wanted to say."

My heart thuds. This explains a lot. Patrick doesn't suddenly have feelings for me, so why did I get a tiny thrill at the thought that he might?

No, I've got to put that out of my mind. The most important thing here has been our friendship. I'm not going to compromise that.

"Okay, well, first of all, I'm sorry you've been feeling this way," I say. "And you're not the only one who has been a jerk lately. I've also been acting stupid. It's so silly, but for some reason, I thought you started liking me. And then I got confused, because why now? When I've *just* started liking someone else? But I'm glad you're being clear about your feelings. It helps me know where you stand."

Patrick smiles, but I swear it looks forced.

"And, you know," I go on, unable to stop these feelings from pouring out of my mouth. "You don't have to worry about any of that, Patrick. You'll always be my best friend, but I hope you understand that when I get a new boyfriend, he probably will become my priority. And that may happen to you too. With whoever you end up dating in the future, you know?"

He opens his mouth like he wants to say something, but then closes it. I take this as a sign to wrap things up, so I rise to my feet. The festival is in two hours. There's a boy who wants to hang out with me all night—one who's led me to believe he may *actually* like me—and I can't waste any more time dillydallying here with Patrick, who only sees me as a friend. His parents should be here any minute. He'll be okay.

"Let me know how the doctor goes, and get some rest, okay? I need to go get ready for the festival." Once I reach the doorway, I turn back to him. "I'll see you at school tomorrow."

And then I scramble out of the nurse's office.

THIRTY-SIX

SARA

I don't stop moving until I'm a good thirty feet away from the nurse's office, then I press my back against the wall and sink onto the floor until I'm sitting on the cold linoleum. I tug my knees into my chest and bury my face into my arms to block out the world around me.

Stupid Patrick. Ugh. I'm supposed to be over him. Aren't I? So why is he getting in my head like this?

I actually convinced myself he was going to tell me he likes me as more than a friend. And what would I have said? I've been so fixated with my crush on Joe, so the ping-ponging in my heart is conflicting. I'm not supposed to feel disappointed by Patrick's lack of feelings toward me. Period, end of discussion.

None of this matters. I'm going out with Joe tonight. Joe, the one who's excited to spend the festival by my side. That's not nothing. It's a huge deal, actually.

But if Patrick doesn't have a crush on me, why would

Joe? How did I think I could have my first kiss with him? I mean, what could he possibly see in me? Not only do I suck at calculus, but I suck at love.

So much for romanticizing my life.

I don't realize I've spoken all of this out loud until I hear shoes squeak to a halt in front of me. Oh no. Someone was listening?

"Did you know the average floor has about seven hundred and sixty-four bacteria per square inch?"

I tilt my gaze up. It's Subwayboy.

He adjusts his frames. "What are you doing on the floor?"

"Oh, you know, just the usual boy problems," I admit, because why lie if he heard it all already? "It can get pretty tough, Subwayboy."

"Please don't start calling me that." Oliver groans, slipping his thumbs under his backpack straps. "And maybe if you start focusing more on important things like your studies, you wouldn't be so worried about trivial things like *boy problems*."

I stand, brushing off whatever dust and floor bacteria might be on my track pants. "Of course. You're right, Subwayboy. You know, you're pretty brainy for a junior." My lips curve into a smile. "Somehow you always seem to know everything, don't you?"

His hand flies to the back of his neck as he averts his gaze to his Sambas. We're matching again. I'm not sure if he notices.

"Not everything," he insists. "Anyway, I'm late for a tutoring appointment. But, uh, did you happen to pass your test?"

That's right. I haven't seen him since lunch, and we hadn't gotten our tests before then.

Grinning, I throw an exuberant thumbs-up right below his chin. "Passed!"

Oliver presses back a smile, which is too bad, because now I know he has a great one.

"Okay, cool," he says, already turning toward the library. "See you tonight."

I watch him go, right until he disappears around the corner. Did Oliver Yang express interest in *me*, Sara Lin? More specifically, did he truly seem to care about my passing grade?

"Huh," I say to myself. "That was random."

"It sure was, Sara Lin."

I just about leap out of my own skin. Lulu's appeared by my side, silent as an avalanche of cotton balls.

"Lulu! Geez, where did you even come from?"

Her silver eyes narrow. "I go to this school."

Not what I meant, but okay.

"By the way, I don't think you should worry."

"Worry?" I repeat.

"About what's lingering on your mind." Her mauve lips remain in a flat line but a coy look dances behind her eyes. "Your first kiss."

Me and my giant mouth. How long was she lurking without making her presence known? She must have heard me going on like some lovesick soap opera actor.

"I sense it will happen very soon," Lulu continues cryptically.

Well, now she has my undivided attention.

"How do you know?" I place my palms on either side of her shoulders, jostling her. "And how soon?"

She gives a little shrug, eyes going glassy with disinterest. "Not sure. Could be tonight. Or it could be tonight of next year. Hard to tell, really."

My heart trips inside my chest. Lulu believes my first kiss might happen tonight!

"Did you say tonight? Tonight's the festival." I release her shoulders. "Could it happen then? With Joseph Yang?"

"Maybe—but a warning before my mysterious departure: Remember my earlier predictions. They may help you figure things out." She takes one step back. "And now I must depart."

With a sudden whirl on her heel, she spins, a cloud of purple smoke unfurling around her, and disappears.

I cough. Blink. Leave it to Lulu to make a mysterious exit.

What was she talking about? Those earlier predictions. Huh. That must have been when she drew my tarot cards in the bathroom.

But—gosh, what *were* those predictions? Something about how someone likes me, and the second one was—what? Stay away from the new kid? What was her last one, then?

Her voice suddenly pops into my head. *You're gonna die.*

My eyes widen. No, hold on. That was the wrong prediction.

Dang it! I should have written them down.

Wait a second, do I even believe anything she says about this kind of stuff? How much can I rely on her vision, really? What am I *thinking*? I don't need her magical prediction to tell me when I should kiss someone.

But if tonight happens to be the big night, I won't be upset.

That's it! I'll take my destiny in my own hands. Romanticizing my life, here I come!

Thanks, Bon Bon. This is a great motivator for me to make a real change in my love life.

Starting tonight.

THIRTY-SEVEN

PATRICK

"What happened to your arm?" Sara's dad asks as he widens the door to let me inside. "Get into a gang fight?"

Okay, maybe coming to Sara's straight from my hospital visit wasn't the best idea—especially with my arm in a noticeable sling—but I hate where our conversation left off. Also? I don't like picturing her walking to the festival alone. I mean, I know Joe and Oliver can walk over with her, but still. She didn't explicitly say that was the plan, so why should I assume?

Her dad raises his eyebrows, waiting for my answer. He's always been a bit intimidating with his thick moustache and stern stare.

"Uh—" I flounder. "Sure?"

"Patrick?"

Sara pokes her head out of her room and—*wow*. She's done her makeup differently, in a way that makes her round amber eyes pop, and there's a warm shimmer dusting her cheeks. It's not too much, but I can't help but blink at her in awe. She looks great.

She glides down the hall until she's next to her dad. "What are you doing here?"

"I'm coming to the festival with you, what do you think?"

As I try to step into her apartment, her dad blocks my path. "Hold on, young man. Tell me more about this gang fight."

"He's kidding, Dad," Sara says, tugging my good arm and pulling me down the hall and into her bedroom. "Of course he's not in a gang."

"Hey! No funny business in there," he shouts after us.

Sara all but shoves me into her room, rolling her eyes as she closes the door to a narrow crack. "Ew, Dad. I'm just finishing my makeup!"

Ew? Should I be offended?

As she shuts her door, I look around. I've been in Sara's room hundreds of times, but today there's a stronger scent of something sweet—like peaches and vanilla undertones. Like her. She's made her bed, lavender comforter neatly tucked in, and I sit on the edge of it as she moves to the mirror hung on the wall behind her dresser. Her makeup is all spread out like it's on a beauty counter.

She reaches for a soft-looking pom-pom that reminds me of a fluffy cloud. "How's your arm?"

"Broken, but it's fine."

In the end, the hospital X-ray proved I had broken my arm, and the doctor said I did a number on my wrist and shoulder, which was dislocated. It hurt like hell when they reset it, so much so that my eyes had teared in pain. Now my arm's in a cast, and I have to decrease mobility in my shoulder for a few weeks, which is why I'm in a sling. They also gave me medication to dull the pain, and that kicked in on the walk over here.

She unclasps a compact and dabs the pom-pom thing on a pink hue. "Oh geez. Are you sure you should go tonight? I mean, aren't you in a lot of pain?"

I'm momentarily mesmerized by the subtle color the blush creates across her cheekbones.

"Uh." I snap out of my trance. "No, not really."

"But shouldn't you rest?"

I adjust the bill on my backward cap. "Resting is overrated. I thought the festival would be more fun than staying home."

"Oh, well, I'm not even sure I'll have time to hang out, Patrick." She's swiping mascara over her eyelashes now, and I have no idea how she does it without blinking or getting it everywhere. That's true talent. "I'm going to be working the festival with the rest of Newspaper Club, probably interviewing a ton of students."

I snort. "Yeah, right. You probably think you're going on a date with Joseph Yang."

The tips of her ears tinge pink, the same color as her blush.

"And that's why you're getting ready like you're attending a ball," I add.

"Okay, yes, there's that too." She combs her fingers through the short ends of her hair. It looks wavier than usual. She must have styled it differently. "But I'm really excited to have my first Newspaper Club assignment. I've been looking forward to it for a while. Seeing my words in print—how cool is that?"

I grab her heart-shaped pillow with my good arm and pull it into my chest. "Fine, fine. As long as you focus on that instead of Goody Two-Shoes Joe."

She whirls on me, hands on her hips. "What's that supposed to mean?"

"What?"

"Why don't you like Joe? He's, like, the nicest guy." She smooths her hands over her butter-yellow skirt, the one with tiny daisies all over. "Earlier you said you were happy for me."

"Nothing," I insist, eyes on her pillow. "I'm just worried about something Rose said earlier about you two, which I think she might be right about—"

Sara frowns. "You're listening to Rose now? Patrick, are you *hearing* yourself?"

"No, listen." My eyes jump to hers. "She had a good point. She said—"

All of a sudden, she slaps a hand to her forehead. "Wait—that's it!"

Huh?

"My prediction," she clarifies, setting down the pom-pom. "I remember it now. Lulu's final tarot prediction was that someone would try and steal my man. That's totally gonna be Rose tonight when I try and get my first kiss from Joe!"

First kiss? From *Joe*? How did we even get here?

And why does it feel like my stomach is twisting into knots?

I sit up straighter. "What are you talking about?"

She comes and sits next to me on her bed, and that's when I notice a pretty peach shimmer on her eyelids. "Lulu made a prediction with her tarot cards. She said someone new had started showing an interest in me," she explains. "Which is Joe!

And then her second prediction was to stay away from the new kid. I'm sure that means Oliver—I can sense he's nothing but trouble. But her last prediction? Someone is going to steal my man. And!" Her eyes widen. "She also said I'm getting my first kiss tonight, and what if all this means Rose is going to mess it up?"

No hate to Lulu, but I'm not sure I buy into her mystical predictions. I thought she did it to make a quick buck off students—which I have to respect—but for her to lead Sara on like this? Nobody can predict when you'll get your first kiss or who might steal your man. It's a bunch of bologna.

"Are you kidding me?"

But it's as if she doesn't hear me. "I have to stay away from Rose," she declares. "No exceptions."

"Sara, you're ridiculous. And what are you talking about—your first kiss with Joe? How is that even going to happen? You barely know him."

Sara crosses her arms, defensive now. "You don't know anything, Patrick. Besides, we're friends now."

With my good hand, I slap a palm to my forehead, exasperated. "Oh my gosh, Sara."

She studies me for so long, I start to feel like I'm bacteria under a microscope. "I know what this is."

My heart drops to my toes. I look at her sidelong, wondering if she can sense my jealousy. Because that's what this is, isn't it? Even though I hate to admit it, I'm jealous of Joe. I mean, when have I ever had the urge to show off in *gym class*, of all places?

Her mouth twists into a sneaky smirk. "You don't think I have the guts."

Oh no. Not this.

I spring to my feet. "No way, I'm not playing this betting game anymore."

She yanks my good arm and tugs me back down onto the bed. "Come on! I thought it was your favorite game."

"Well, it becomes less exciting when I keep winning every time."

She drops her hand from my arm, but there's a fire in her eyes. "You're not winning this one. I have a really good feeling about tonight."

"Sara, you say that *every* time. So, no. I'm not agreeing to this."

And then I get up again, moving before she can stop me, and head for her door.

"Whatever, who's chicken now?" she calls after me. "I'm still getting my first kiss tonight anyway, no matter what."

This makes me pause. I hang my head. Why did I have to bet her to kiss Subwayboy in the first place? Now she won't let it go until she does win. So I've got to say something that makes her back down from this bet. Give her something she'd never in a million years agree to.

Slowly, I turn around and face her. "You really want to do this?"

She lifts her chin in determination. That's enough of an answer.

"Fine, if you don't get your first kiss by the end of the festival tonight," I say, "you'll have to quit Newspaper Club."

I expect her to backtrack right away. *Actually, Patrick, we better not bet tonight! Let fate work its magic instead!* Because if she loves writing so much, why would she agree if there's a fifty-fifty chance she'll have to give it up? She wouldn't. End of story.

Instead, her eyes widen in surprise. Then she's on her feet, grabbing her purse and thick wool cardigan from her closet before spinning back around.

"Okay, deal," she says merrily, as though I've offered her a bucket of chocolate candy. She's already heading for the door. "Ah, this is so exciting! Let's go!"

My heart just about stops. She's serious? No—she wasn't supposed to agree!

"Wait! I thought you love Newspaper Club?"

"Right," she agrees. "So it's just more motivation to not fail since I *do* love it."

I slide between her and the door, blocking her exit. "Exactly, so don't throw it away for a stupid bet."

She looks me up and down, hands on her hips. "It's not stupid. I just told you—I need motivation to help me go through with it."

Now it makes sense. Assuming Sara would back down from a high-stakes bet was the wrong move. Instead, I've inadvertently added more fuel to her fire. She can't lose tonight because, now, the thing she loves most is on the line.

"Fine." I offer her a hand, and she shakes it. "Your loss."

"Unless I win." She steps around me and throws open her door. "And remember, don't listen to Rose. And stay away from Subwayboy. Oh—and!" She cups her face and grins. "Kiss Joseph Yang!"

I reel back, making a face like I've just tasted bad fish. "Do I have to?"

"Me! I kiss Joe, not you." She laughs as she skip out of her room. "Now let's go already! Vicky's already on her way. And the Yangs are waiting for us outside."

I'm following behind her, but stop in my tracks when the last thing she said registers in my brain. "The Yangs? As in—*plural*?"

"Oh, didn't you know?" She tosses a sly smile over her shoulder. "Oliver and Joe are brothers."

THIRTY-EIGHT

SARA

In only a few hours, Eagle Gate High School's faculty, with the help from each grade's student council, has completely transformed the track field into a festival wonderland.

Booths with pitched canvas awnings are lined in tidy rows with enough room for students to walk comfortably on either side. Blue and silver pennant banners crisscross overhead, promoting our school colors, and balloon clusters are arranged beside every other booth to add flair. Hand-painted signs are secured to the top of every booth, clearly labeled for students as they peruse the options. There's a waft of marinara in the air—probably from the free pizza they're giving out—and something sweet, like fried dough. I've never been an active member of a club during a festival night, so it feels extra exciting.

It's easy to spot the Newspaper Club booth. Not because it's fancy or done up or anything, but because Mickey Dean is yelling so enthusiastically, you'd think money had just started raining from the sky.

"Hey! *Oliver!* Hey, guys, over here!"

Joe had talked to me the entire walk over, sharing how excited he was to work on our first story together. I'd flushed crimson under the moonlight, because I was equally thrilled. Which is why I have to make sure I spend the entire night with him. We're friends now, aren't we? We've had multiple conversations, have common interests, and are even in the same club. I just know there's some romantic opportunity waiting for us at the festival. I can practically feel it in the way my skin hums with anticipation.

Joe turns to his brother, pressing back a smile. "Someone's excited to see you."

Oliver sighs, which is cut short when Mickey Dean tears away from the booth and bear tackles him into a hug.

Mickey Dean squeezes tighter. "Olly boy!"

Patrick leans next to my ear. "'Olly boy'? More like Subwayboy."

I snort. "That's not even funny, Patrick."

"Then why did you snort-laugh?"

Oliver glares at us as Mickey Dean releases him. Whoops. Were we that loud?

"Nice of you to *finally* show up," Rose says, a bite to her tone.

Of course she looks perfect. I bet she didn't even try that hard either. She's wearing a gorgeous plaid peacoat in various shades of pink, which she's paired with an expensive-looking cream turtleneck sweaterdress. Lips glossed, hair shiny as ever.

"Sorry we're a bit late," Joe offers, one hand nervously smoothing the back of his hair.

"It's fine, but we should go ahead and get started."

I'm about to ask what I can do to help when, from my periphery, I spot a familiar face. "Vicky!" I exclaim, throwing my arms around her. "I feel like I haven't seen you in forever."

She laughs. "Hey, Sara."

It's so good to see her. There's no time to fill her in on the kiss bet, but her presence helps calm my nerves. When I let go, she grins at everyone as she adjusts the lavender scarf secured around her neck. Joe shifts closer to us, waving to her in polite greeting. She waves back.

"Okay, no time to lose, everyone," Rose commands, all business. "Mickey Dean and Cordelia, you're on photojournalism duty. Get good pictures. Oliver, you'll stay at the booth and pass out pamphlets. And Joe"—I swear her eyes sparkle—"you and I will get these interviews."

Conversation breaks out among the group. Everyone starts walking their separate ways, but I clear my throat.

"Uh, do I have a job?"

Rose looks like she just found gum at the bottom of her shoe. "Oh—Sara. Just stay and help Oliver in the booth. You'll both be in charge of gathering new sign-ups."

"What?" I blurt. "No!"

Oliver's eyes snap to mine, and his lips tug down in an annoyed frown. I don't mean to offend him, but hanging with Oliver all night isn't part of my plan. How is Joe supposed to want to kiss me if he's with Rose all evening? There's no way an opportunity will come up if we're not together.

Not only that, but how am I supposed to write my first published article if I can't do any student interviews? I've been itching to write something—to actually get my work out there and read by people. I was excited to show my dad, even! Am I supposed to go home and tell him I passed around pamphlets all night instead of dipping my toes in real journalism?

Rose scoffs. "What, do you have a problem with Oliver?"

"Uh, no?" I shake my head. "I mean, of course not. I just thought I'd get a chance to interview students too. I even prepared questions, just like you asked."

She heaves a dramatic sigh, like I'm the unreasonable one here. "Sara, just stay at the booth."

But I won't back down. Not on what's supposed to be the most important night of my romantic life. "I don't think the booth needs two people—"

"Can't you do as you're told?" Rose says, fully aggravated now. "I'm president, which means I'm the one who gives assignments. From now on, try not to fight me on my decisions."

"Um." Joe's eyes skip from me to Rose, as if he's trying to come up with a peacekeeping idea. "What if we, uh, rotate? Maybe Rose and I can do interviews for a bit, then we'll come back and switch? That sounds fair, right, Rose?"

"Okay, sure, whatever." Rose threads her arm through his, then leads Joe away from us. "We don't have time for this, let's go."

But right before they disappear from sight, Rose tosses a conniving look over her shoulder. One that's directed right at Patrick. His gaze drops to his sneakers, as if he hopes no one caught that. Unfortunately for him, I'm observant tonight. I *knew* they were up to something! Those scheming schemers.

I spin on my heel, facing him. "What was that look?"

Patrick palms the back of his neck uneasily. "Uh, who knows? She's probably in love with me or something."

Psh, yeah right. It's obvious Rose set all this up to have alone time with Joe. If she was *actually* into Patrick, she'd have his arm—well, his good one, anyway—threaded through hers right now.

Patrick can sense I'm about to prod him until he tells me the truth, so he grabs Vicky's hand. "Let's go check out the festival, Vicky. I'm not gonna hang out at this boring booth all night."

"Oh, uh"—Vicky throws me an apologetic look as she's tugged away—"sorry, Sara! I'll come back soon, I promise."

I step forward but Patrick's keen on keeping a fast pace. Too bad he didn't sprain his ankle instead. He'd be much easier to catch. "Wait! Don't leave me alone here with—"

I stop in my tracks, my eyes jumping to Oliver, who's already taken a seat in a folding chair behind the booth. A hand cups his jaw, and his bored stare lingers on me like he'd really love to know the end of my sentence.

"—all this work!" I improvise. "Geez, so much *work* at the booth."

Without much of a choice, I head behind the booth and sit in the only empty chair beside Oliver, sighing. I organize the twenty or so pamphlets in front of us into a neat pile, then cast my gaze into the crowd. Students huddle together in clusters, squealing excitedly as they point where they should go next. No one comes over to chat with us.

Well, I have two options. Talk to Oliver, or get to work on gathering signatures.

I choose the lesser of two evils.

I snatch a pamphlet from my pile and wave it into the air. "Come join Newspaper Club! Learn all about the importance of journalism! Hey, you!" A freshman pretends like he didn't just make eye contact with me and scurries away. "Don't you want some adventure in your life?"

As it turns out, he does not. Because he only walks faster, not looking back.

I go on like this for another ten minutes, but no one comes around. Not even a polite no thanks. Was Patrick right? Does anyone really care about newspaper?

Eventually I give in, slumping back in my seat. Oliver adjusts the collar of his vintage bomber jacket, which has this cool sherpa lining, and continues ignoring me.

"What's the point?" I grumble. "Ugh, I can't believe I'm stuck doing this. They totally ditched us here."

Oliver offers no response, just keeps his eyes locked on his phone screen.

"My time is running out. Worse? I can't even enjoy the festival because I'm stuck here." I sound whiny, like I'm on the verge of a tantrum, but I don't care. Rose got her way, like she always does. "And there's nothing we can do about it."

Faint, muffled music sounds from beside me. When I glance over, I realize why. Oliver's wearing his earbuds. Guess he wasn't listening to me lament. Or maybe he was and decided to tune me out, which is the more Oliver thing to do, if I'm being honest.

I glance down at his screen. Guns N' Roses.

I tap my finger near his phone to grab his attention. "Fun choice."

Disbelief is splayed across his face as he removes an earbud. "You listen to Guns N' Roses?"

"*You* listen to Guns N' Roses?" I fire back. "Never picked

you for a classic rock kinda guy. Mozart? Sure. Chopin? Definitely. Or maybe a math podcast—"

"Who listens to math podcasts?" he says, incredulous. "Boring."

"Right? Maybe I would, though, if I was having trouble falling asleep."

The corners of his mouth rise, just slightly, but I catch it. Wow, did Oliver and I just agree about something? How unlike us.

"How'd you get into Guns N' Roses, anyway?"

He looks at me sidelong. "I like music that's guitar-forward."

Joe told me he was saving up for a guitar. I wonder if he already plays. Maybe he wants to start taking lessons. Ha, what if my dad gave him guitar lessons in exchange for my calculus tutoring? On second thought, no way. Inviting Oliver into my apartment? Bad idea. So bad it might just give me nightmares.

"They're fine, I guess," I say. "My dad listens to them all the time. All those classics, really. Led Zeppelin, AC/DC, Queen—he's been trying to drill them into my head for years."

"Do you—like it?" Oliver says cautiously, then clarifies. "That kinda music?"

"Eh, I don't know. Some of it's good, but generally, it's a bit heavy for my taste."

"It's not all heavy." Oliver searches for something on Spotify. "Let me show you a really good one. Here."

He doesn't glance up at me as he offers me his earbud dangling from the wire, just holds it out and waits for me to accept.

I hesitate. "Uh, that's okay."

Now his eyes meet mine. "Come on, it's just a song."

And before I know what's happening, he sticks it in my ear. I have to scoot a little closer so the cord tension doesn't stretch, and once I'm settled, he taps Play.

It's another Guns N' Roses song, and when I glance at his screen, I find the title: "Patience." It doesn't start out guns blazing—pun intended—but acoustic. Slow and a little sad, but sweet and hopeful at the same time. The lyrics are about missing a girl and needing patience in order to make things right.

And . . . I don't hate it.

When it ends, I meet his eyes. "Not bad."

Oliver smiles, a real smile with dimples appearing on both cheeks, and my heart suddenly skips like a record. It happens so fast I think I've imagined it.

Blinking this reaction away, I gesture to his phone. "Okay, what are your thoughts on Queen?"

Oliver's eyes flash with excitement. "I actually *really* like Queen."

"Me too. What's your favorite song?"

As he thinks, he cups his chin in his palm. "Probably 'Don't Stop Me Now.'"

"Oh, that's a good one." His phone still sits on the table between us, so I tap the screen to navigate to the search bar. "I'll show you my favorite."

"Don't tell me it's 'Bohemian Rhapsody.'"

"Hey, nothing wrong with that, Music Snob—"

"*Please* don't start calling me that. It's bad enough you call me Subwayboy."

"Because you *are* Subwayboy. But no, it's not 'Rhapsody.'" The opening of "Killer Queen" begins. "It's this one."

Oliver's gaze clings to mine. "That's my second favorite."

"Sometimes I think my dad keeps his moustache because he thinks it makes him look like Freddie Mercury," I say.

Oliver laughs—a real, genuine laugh! "I'm going to tell him he does the next time I see him in the hall."

I guess I shouldn't be surprised he's crossed paths with my dad, given that we live five feet from each other, but I am.

"Don't. If you do, he will never shut up about it, and then I will have to hear about it every day of my life until I die."

This time, Oliver's eyes crinkle when he laughs. "I'm playing you my favorite Bowie song after this, and then you can play me yours."

It's strange. I don't think I've seen Oliver this happy, well, ever. Even stranger? I'm sort of enjoying this.

"Okay," I say, grinning. "Deal."

THIRTY-NINE

PATRICK

I've been wandering around the festival with Vicky for almost two hours. We got distracted by the Bake Club's pie-eating contest for a good while before we left to grab a slice of free pizza. I assumed Sara Lin would text me once Rose released her from newspaper booth duty, but she hasn't. Which means she's probably already wandered off with Joe.

Ugh, figures.

At least I have Vicky to keep me company. We've already compared Eagle Gate's clubs and extracurriculars to the ones she has at Brookside, but she was eager to learn more about the organizations they don't have—like Culinary Club. She spends so much time working at Kiki's, so I don't get why she'd want to surround herself with even more food, but I oblige anyway. It's not like I have anything better to do.

Eventually, the pain meds my doctor gave me at the hospital start wearing off. I start moving slower, and Vicky offers to meet me back at the booth after she finds me some water. It's a kind gesture, really, so I tell her I'll meet her over there.

When I enter the booth from the back, I'm shocked to find the back of Sara Lin's head, where she's sitting next to—

Subwayboy?

What the heck? Have they been here this entire time? Where's Joe?

I drag another folding chair between them, which makes them jolt apart. Ah. They were listening to music with his earphones. They've folded their jackets over the backs of their chairs, comfortable, as if they've been here a while.

Weird. Since when are they friendly? Doesn't matter, though I guess it's a good thing I didn't bet her she'd sit here in silence the entire time.

"Patrick? Are you okay?"

But it's not Sara who asks. It's Tammy.

Where did she even come from?

I sink into the chair. "My pain meds wore off. Vicky went to grab water for me."

Sara checks the time on Oliver's phone. "It's okay, Patrick. The festival's almost over. You can—" Suddenly, her face falls. "Crap! The festival's almost over!"

I arch one brow. "You *just* said that."

She's on her feet in an instant, scrambling toward the front of the booth. "Why didn't Rose ever come back? Ugh!"

I give her my best conspiratorial grin. "Twenty minutes until you've gotta quit Newspaper Club *forever*."

Oliver jolts upright, concern flashing in his eyes as he looks to Sara. "What?"

Sara grabs her head between her palms, clearly in distress about this. "Agh, I lost track of time!"

Tammy clears her throat, startling me all over again. I already forgot she was standing behind me.

"Well, if you need to go, maybe Patrick and I can stay here and tend the booth for you guys?" Tammy suggests.

Relief floods Sara's face. "That would be amazing—*thank you*, Tammy."

As she's pulling on her cardigan, I narrow my eyes at her. "Just give up, Sara. It's too late. How are you even going to find them? This field is huge. Vicky and I didn't even make it to all the booths."

"It's not too late," she snaps, frustrated. "I have twenty minutes."

An annoyed ache spreads through my chest. I fiddle with the strap of my sling, which is folded over my jean jacket like a seat belt.

I'm conflicted. Sure, I want Sara to win the bet so she can stay in Newspaper Club, but I'm jealous she's about to get her first kiss from Joe. Ugh! I don't even want to imagine it.

"Then hurry up and go," I mumble under my breath.

"Twenty minutes for what?" Oliver asks, coming around to Sara's side. "Did you two make another stupid bet?"

Sara blushes. "Uh, maybe?"

Oliver pulls on his jacket. "Fine. I'll help you. Let's go."

"Oh—you don't have to! It's okay, really," Sara argues, but Oliver's already placed two hands on her back, gently guiding her away from the booth.

"Nineteen minutes," Oliver warns, like he's Father Time himself. "For whatever it is you have to do. So let's go."

Sara throws me a helpless look over her shoulder as they take off, but what does she expect me to do? Tammy already volunteered us to stay.

Speaking of, Tammy slips into the empty seat next to me. Her signature pigtails hang over her cashmere sweater, and she stares at me from behind her round glasses.

I slap a hand to my forehead, suddenly frustrated. "Dang it, if she can't find him, she's gonna lose again and it'll be all my fault," I moan. "Why did I agree to this?"

Tammy fixes me with a sympathetic look. "What's the bet about?"

"She has to kiss someone by the end of the festival, so now she's going to find my arch nemesis Joseph L. Yang." I hinge over the table, clutching my head with my good arm, then add, "The *L* stands for loser."

"Oh," Tammy says, voice quiet.

"She's probably going to get rejected by him," I go on. "And I still can't decide if it's a good thing or a bad thing. Probably bad, right? Ugh, yeah. I know. I'm so stupid. Why would I bet her to kiss someone else if I like her? I mean, if she wanted to get her first kiss over with so badly, I should have just bet her to kiss *me*."

Tammy gasps and throws her hand over her mouth. "Patrick!"

"I mean—I don't know what I'm saying. I can't think when I'm in pain," I say, face flaming.

Argh, why did I just say all that to Tammy? What if she tells Sara?

After a long pause, Tammy says, "Patrick, if you like her so much, shouldn't you go and stop her?"

Do I like her? Those words slid from my mouth so easily, which has to mean *something*. Right? Joe's a great guy, but when I picture Sara with a boyfriend it's . . .

Me.

But do I want to ruin what we have? What does it mean for our friendship?

"I give up." I groan into my arm. "It's too late."

"It's *not* too late."

But that wasn't Tammy's voice. I lift my head to find Rose coming toward us.

"Where the heck have you been?" I blurt.

Rose rolls her eyes, her tall suede boots emphasizing each step she takes until she stops at the table. "Joe and I were interviewing students, remember? He's such a great interviewer, by the way." She practically swoons when she says this. "And he said I have amazing skills, too, which I already knew, but it's nice to hear."

I adjust my hat with my good arm as my broken arm flares with pain. I wince, then say, "So, what, are you two dating now or something?"

Rose flushes. "If you *must* know, I admitted that I'm into him and asked when he was going to ask me out. Obviously, we'd make a cute couple."

"Oh, Rose, that's so exciting!" Tammy squeaks. "So you're a couple now?"

Her blush deepens. "Not exactly." She clears her throat. "He got all blustery and awkward and started apologizing, so then I jumped to the next best conclusion. I mean, he's so nice and good-looking. Gentle, respectful, with amazing hair and great fashion sense—"

I release an aggravated sigh, because I don't want to hear about how great Joe is right now. "Get to the point."

Rose narrows her eyes at me. "So I said, 'You're gay, aren't you?'"

"Joe's *gay*?" Tammy and I gasp in unison.

Wow, talk about a plot twist.

"That's the thing—he's not!" she confirms. "This is what I've been trying to tell you this whole time, *geez*. If you really don't want to lose Sara Lin, you need to stop her right now."

I raise my brows. "What are you *talking* about?"

"Joe told me he already likes someone else. Another girl, he said," Rose continues, a wash of insecurity creasing across her forehead. "And I was like, *Well, you need to be more careful and direct with your feelings, Joe! If you keep treating all these girls the same, how are they supposed to know if you like them or not?*" She crosses her arms. "And he told me I was right! That he *should* be more direct. And then he decided he would confess to her—*tonight*."

Unease shifts in my stomach. "Well, who's he confessing to?"

"Isn't it obvious? Patrick, Joe's going to confess his feelings for Sara." Irritation flicks behind her eyes. "And you know what? It's probably good Sara's left the booth. Joe thinks she's still here, so it'll be the first place he looks. Which means one of us needs to go find her and stall her before he turns up. And it would be perfect if you use that time to tell her how you feel, Patrick. That way you can keep her mind off Joe."

I launch to my feet, slamming a palm on the table to stabilize myself. "Stop saying all this like I'm working with you! I'm not going along with your evil master plan to split them up. I already told you, I'm not doing *any of this* for you."

Rose's lips puff into a pout, her eyes narrowing as she scrutinizes me. "Whatever, Patrick. The thing is, whichever way you look at it, it doesn't matter. We both want the same thing in the end."

Tammy rises to her feet, then gives me an encouraging nod. I take a deep breath. Okay. It's official. Joe has a crush on Sara. So if I'm going to explore something deeper than friendship with her, I need to tell her that my feelings have changed. And I have to do it *tonight*. No regrets, no mistakes.

I glance around, wondering if Vicky's going to show up with my water. I really don't want to ditch her, but I'm running out of time. It's fine, I decide. She'll text me to figure out where I've gone, and then I can tell her everything. Because she was right all along, wasn't she? I needed to figure out my feelings toward Sara before she fully moved on.

"Hurry," Rose snaps. "You guys go that way, and I'll go this way."

I grasp Tammy's hand with my good hand. "Fine," I say, already moving away from Rose. "Text me as soon as you find her."

And as we tear down the rows of booths, I find myself hoping I'm not too late.

FORTY

SARA

Above us, the night sky is full of twinkling stars that poke against its dark contrast. Students weave around us, racing toward a booth that offers a cornhole game. I slide my hands into the pocket of my camel-colored cardigan, and tuck them into balls to keep them warm. The temperature's dipped only slightly, but it's enough to send a slight chill through me.

Oliver and I have been speed walking in silence for at least a minute. He's let me take the lead, following along behind me as I scan the crowd, hoping to find Joe's tall head among the sea of bodies.

"So you're not going to tell me what this whole bet thing is about?"

No, Subwayboy, I won't. Because—ack! How did I lose track of time? It had felt like we'd gone back and forth over our personal music taste for ten minutes, but that somehow had morphed into two hours. Two! I hadn't even realized we'd been chatting for so long, but it'd felt . . . effortless? The opposite of how I feel every time I have to do math in his presence, really. Dare I say *fun*?

I had no idea Oliver knew so much about music and chord progressions and random facts about Metallica and the Eagles, and I think I surprised him with how many Led Zeppelin songs I'm familiar with. At one point we'd both even played the air guitar. *Together*.

Is this the twilight zone?

"It's embarrassing," I admit, staring straight ahead. "So, no."

Oliver lets out an aggravated breath and shoves his hands into his jacket pockets. "Then how am I supposed to help you?"

"Why are you so persistent about this?" I counter. "I never even asked for your help. Besides, it's not something you can help me out with, exactly."

"What, you have to find another random stranger to kiss?"

My blush deepens. "Of course not."

Not a stranger, I think, *just your brother*.

"There you are!"

Oliver and I swivel around to find Rose jogging over to us.

"I've been looking all over for you," she continues, slightly out of breath. "Why did you guys leave the booth? I need—"

"*No*, Rose," I say firmly, finally growing that backbone I needed all along. "I'm not going back to sit in the booth. The festival's practically over. You said you'd switch with us and you never did."

"I don't care about that. Actually, I don't need you at the booth." Her eyes land on the massive school lurking behind us. "I need you two to—uh, get more pamphlets from the classroom!"

"*What?*" I splutter. "Rose, there are zillions at the booth already."

"Just hurry up," she orders. "This is the most crucial time of the festival. We have to give them out before everyone goes home."

Oliver looks to the sky and releases a massive sigh. I don't blame him. I'm over her too.

"That doesn't even make any sense, Rose," I argue.

"Whatever, let's just go." Oliver places his hands on my back, moving us away from the festival and heading toward the paved pathway that leads back to the school.

I meet him with resistance. "But—"

"She's not going to change her mind," Oliver mutters in my ear as Rose watches us leave, a smug smile toying on her lips. "May as well be quick so we can get back to—whatever you're doing."

This is a *disaster*. Never in my wildest dreams did I imagine I'd mess tonight up this badly. I spent exactly zero minutes with Joe during the festival, and now I'm about to lose this bet because I'm on a hunt for stupid pamphlets.

But I allow Oliver to guide me inside, because what else can I do?

It's quiet once we enter the building. I don't think I've ever been at school this late, and it feels weird, like I've stepped into the bathtub with shoes on. Most of the fluorescents are turned off, but we don't have to worry, because the windows invite in light from the lampposts right outside.

Oliver leads us up the stairs to Mrs. Huber's classroom. She teaches all the journalism classes and keeps excess materials stored inside. It's also where Newspaper Club meets.

"I still think this makes zero sense," I mutter as we climb.

"Rose is gonna do what Rose wants," Oliver says. "Anyway, maybe if you told me what you have to do, I'd be able to help you."

"Just forget it. What's the point?"

Oliver reaches the landing first and waits for me to catch up. Once I do, we start down the hall.

"I can't do it anymore," I continue. "There's no time left. Rose ruined everything, just like Lulu predicted. I didn't listen to anything she said, and now it's too late. Besides, I couldn't go through with it, anyway. It was hard enough with a stranger. Stupid of me to think I'd be brave enough to go for it with someone I have a crush on."

Oliver, who's been walking several steps ahead of me this whole time, turns around. "So you're . . . doing another kiss bet?"

We reach the classroom, and he holds the door open for me. I step inside to avoid answering, but when he comes in after me, it's clear he's waiting for me to reply.

"Uh," I say. "Maybe?"

"And if you don't do it," he continues, piecing everything together, "you have to quit Newspaper Club."

"Agh—yes, okay? That's it." I turn toward the boxes of pamphlets stacked on Mrs. Huber's desk. "It sounds stupid when you put it like that."

"That's because it *is* stupid." Oliver gives me one of his signature judgmental stares from behind his glasses. "Why do you keep making these kiss bets? Just get a boyfriend like every other girl."

Um, hello? Has he met me? What, does he think that I'm

turning down guys left and right? I'm not perfect Rose with great hair and fantastic people skills. I mean, she could hold a conversation with a rock and make it seem cool and interesting.

Heat rushes up my neck and sinks into my cheeks. "I know it's dumb, okay? It doesn't matter anymore, anyway. I already lost because I'm up here with you instead of—"

"Okay, hear me out," Oliver interrupts. "Is it that bad if you lose and have to quit? It might be better that way, right? So you can focus on your grades?" He paws through the boxes, slapping stacks of pamphlets on the desk. "And aren't you going to start taking your college entrance exams soon, anyway?"

I run a hand though my hair. "Yeah, but that's beside the point."

"It's not beside the point, Sara Lin." He looks at me now, those green eyes tangling with mine. "There are more important things than having your first kiss *right this second*. You should worry about things like college entrance exams and passing calculus. I mean, you've been wasting time focusing on Newspaper Club instead of tutoring, and it's affecting your grades."

I cast my gaze to the ground, staring at the cute boots I'd picked out especially for tonight. Proof of what he's saying. And he's right. He's *been* right this whole time, from the very first conversation we had about my priorities. I've been so consumed by my crush on Joe that it's all I've been fixated on. I haven't done a single thing for Newspaper Club tonight. I can't write an article from nothing.

"But I mean—it's not the end of the world." He must sense I'm upset because his voice turns softer. Kinder. "I can always tutor you again even if you lose the bet, unless you really wanna stay in the club and make time for both. I'm sure Patrick would understand and let the whole thing go. It's not like it's a legally binding contract or anything."

"No, you're right. I should just focus on tutoring," I say, letting that dejected feeling spread through me. "It's for the best. I wanted to join newspaper for the wrong reasons at first, anyway. I mostly did it to impress your brother, but he didn't even notice me. And why would he? I'm a mess and a terrible writer."

"No—that's not what I said," Oliver says, confusion blanketing his face. "You're not getting the point."

Suddenly, a voice booms from down the hall. "Here! This one's the journalism classroom. I'd love to show you—"

Oliver and I look at each other. My heart thuds frantically. Joe? What in the world is he doing here? And—oh no. He must be with someone if he's talking to them. But who?

It doesn't matter. I've got to disappear, pronto! Because I'm more confused than ever, and I can't face Joe if I don't even know what I want at this point. It doesn't make me a chicken if I need more time, I decide.

"It's your brother," I say. "He's coming. Quick, hide!"

His brows furrow. "Why?"

But before he can protest further, I tug him behind Mrs. Huber's single pedestal desk and yank him to the floor, forcing him to crouch beneath the surface with me.

The three walls block us from view, like a cramped fortress. Our shoulders bump as we adjust to the tight space. He opens his mouth as if to chastise me, but I slap a hand over it to muffle whatever he's going to say.

And then two sets of footsteps enter the classroom.

FORTY-ONE
PATRICK

"Hey, you! Have you seen Sara Lin?" A sophomore boy shakes his head before wandering off in the opposite direction. "Really? Short, ginger, still looks twelve-years-old?"

From beside me, Tammy lowers her phone from her ear. "She's not answering her phone."

"Dang it." I moan. "Time is running out. Where is she?"

Tammy and I have been frantically searching the festival for Sara, but there's no sign of her or Oliver, who you think would be easier to spot since he's much taller than her. Twinkle lights from each booth light our path as we hustle past crowds of students. I try not to jostle my arm as we jog, because the extra movement doesn't help with the pain.

"Patrick, there you are."

Rose, her hands tucked in the pockets of her peacoat, is quickly walking toward us. She's not with Sara, which means she also hasn't had any luck finding her.

Great.

Tammy and I pause so she can catch up to us, but I've reached my last thread of patience. "What do you *want*, Rose? Still haven't found your stupid boyfriend, Joe Loser Yang?"

"*Patrick*," she huffs, indignant.

"Kidding," I supply weakly.

"Whatever, I'm just trying to tell you I sent her to the journalism classroom." Rose rolls her eyes. "Go stall her there while I keep looking for Joe."

Tammy grabs my good arm and pulls me toward the school. "Great, thanks, Rose!"

I slip from her grasp and twist toward Rose, eyes narrowing. "Fine, but again, I'm *not* doing this for you."

"Sure." Rose flips her hair over her shoulder then heads in the opposite direction.

As Tammy and I dart toward the school's entrance, I wonder what I'm even doing right now. Agh, this pain medication is making my brain loopy. I can't think straight. All I know is, I'm not one of Rose's minions she can boss around.

Okay, Patrick. *Think*. Do I want to stall Sara? If I do, that also means I'm stalling her potential kiss with Joe tonight, which means she loses our kiss bet. Gah, what kind of friend would I be if I let that happen?

Then there's the other problem. If Rose intercepts Joe before he can confess his feelings, Sara still loses the bet. She'll be devastated if she has to quit newspaper.

Ugh! I never thought in a million years she'd agree to this bet. Why did she have to say yes? It only increases the pressure tenfold.

But, hold on—there's a chance Rose doesn't find Joe, isn't there? Joe could be on his way to the journalism classroom *right now* to confess to Sara. And if that's the case, maybe I can intercept Joe! Yeah, that's it! I'll find him before he finds Sara, and then I'll—what? Force him to kiss her so Sara can win the bet? Sure, that works.

Only, what if Joe's not by the classroom? Maybe I can find some other random guy to kiss her so she doesn't lose the bet. Except—didn't Sara tell me she wanted her first kiss to be with someone she really liked? *Loved*, even? Will this plan even work?

Eh, I'll figure it out as I go.

Suddenly, I remember something I read in her blog. How she'd wanted a change this year. To go after what she wanted without fear. Meanwhile, I hadn't wanted anything to change between us because I was comfortable with how things were, and then Joseph Yang threw a wrench in that. Except . . .

It's not really Joe's fault, is it? Even if Joe doesn't confess his feelings to Sara tonight, our friendship will eventually change if one of us starts dating someone. That's inevitable. Did I expect her to never move on and have a crush on somebody else? Of course that was going to happen. Joe just happened to be that person.

I stop in my tracks. Tammy whirls around to face me.

"Why don't you make sure she's not in line to get free ice cream?" I say. "If I don't find her here, I'll text you."

Tammy gives an eager nod. "Good luck!"

I force a smile. She has no idea how much I need it.

But now I know what I have to do.

FORTY-TWO

SARA

I remove my hand from Oliver's mouth and press my finger to my lips, silently pleading for him to stay quiet. His head is bent at an awkward angle to avoid hitting the underside of the desk, and he carefully tries to adjust without accidentally elbowing me.

"Wow, your classrooms are way bigger here."

Wait, that's Vicky's voice! She's here with Joe? How did that happen?

"Yeah, probably because there's a ton more students at Eagle Gate," Joe replies.

Oliver pulls his long legs toward his torso, then rests his chin on his knee as he peers at me, hair falling into his eyes as his head dips. I switch positions and crouch on my knees so I can steal a tiny glance around the workstation.

Vicky and Joe stride toward the window, then stop to face each other. They're still wearing their jackets, cheeks tinged rosy from the outside chill, so they must have just gotten here. But why are they *here* together?

I tuck myself back behind the desk.

"Where do you sit?" Vicky asks.

"Usually right here, next to Sara."

I swallow. From beside me, Oliver peers at me through his eyelashes. He looks so uncomfortable hunched over like that. He's probably gonna send me his chiropractor bill after this.

"Actually, Vicky, I brought you here because I needed to tell you something."

"Oh." There's a note of surprise in her voice. "Okay, what is it?"

"Um, I know I don't go to Brookside High anymore," Joe begins. "But you've been the one I liked the whole time I went there."

My cheeks flame, and I slap my hands over my mouth to withhold a gasp.

"I was too scared to approach you because your beauty is so intimidating," Joe continues. "And I know we just officially met and you don't know me that well, but I've always admired you from afar. So, I guess I was just wondering if you like me too?"

I close my eyes, mortified, as my heat plummets to my toes. This whole time Joe's had a crush on my cousin? Gah, I can't believe I didn't see the signs. Is that why he'd asked if she was coming to the festival when I went over to study? Oh no—is this the only reason he cared if I passed my calculus test?

No, no, no! Don't think like that, Sara.

Joe's always been encouraging, even before he knew Vicky was my cousin. I know better than anyone that you can't help you who have a crush on.

"I do," Vicky blurts, but then immediately backtracks. "I mean—no! No, I can't. I'm so sorry." There's a sound of footsteps rushing toward the door. "Sara's not just my cousin. She's my best friend, and I can't do this to her. I mean, *agh*—she's had the biggest crush on you since you transferred."

I bury my face in my hands to avoid looking at Oliver, but I feel the heat of his gaze blazing into me.

"Sara?" Joe repeats.

"Oh gosh, what am I doing? I wasn't supposed to say that," Vicky says, flustered. "I'm sorry. I can't do this."

Her footsteps retreat, quickly followed by Joe's.

"Wait, Vicky. Hold on—"

The door swings closed with a soft click.

From right next to me, Oliver shifts in place. I can't look at him, because what do I even say? I can't believe he heard all that! Why is my life one big catastrophe?

"This is so embarrassing," I blurt, because I have to say *something.* My hands move to the sides of my face, pressing against my temples. "I can't believe Vicky told Joe and—agh! I've officially lost the stupid bet with Patrick. Joe was my only chance to get a kiss tonight."

From my periphery, I see Oliver reach out to pat my shoulder. His hand sort of lingers in the air, never coming into contact. "Hey—"

"I'm so stupid to have thought Joe liked me." I stare at the floor, my blush deepening. "He liked Vicky this whole time, and not only that, but she likes him too. And who the heck am I to try and stop their love? How ridiculous would that be?"

"Sara—"

But I can't stop the verbal onslaught of feelings that tumble from my lips. "I don't fit into the picture anymore. All because of Lulu's magical prediction, which led me to think I could have my first kiss tonight. How am I so gullible? I don't think there's any hope for me. I'm officially the dumbest person on the planet. And, *ugh*, you're right." I brave a glance at Oliver, who's untucked his head from under the table and let his knees fall to the side on the floor. "I need to stop thinking about romanticizing my life and focus on my real problems."

Suddenly, Oliver reaches out and places both hands on my shoulders. "Sara, stop—just, stop!"

He slides closer to me—not thinking about his floor bacteria facts right now, I guess—and latches his gaze on mine. We're close, I realize. So close that I can smell his citrusy shampoo and the soft cotton fragrance that lingers on his jacket, probably from his laundry detergent.

"You're fine. It's all fine," he says gently. "You're not the dumbest person on this planet, okay? If anyone's dumb, it's my brother for not noticing you this whole time. I mean, he's a great brother. And a really good person, but honestly? He can be so clueless sometimes." He pushes his glasses up the bridge of his nose. "And you're not stupid, either, okay? You're pretty and smart—you just use your intelligence for things you like best, like newspaper! I mean, clearly that's important to you besides whatever reason led you there to begin with, right?"

My eyes widen in surprise, because I'm not used to Oliver saying such nice things about me. Who is this boy and what did he do with the grouch that normally inhabits his body?

"And if you want to stay in the club, um . . ." He swallows, looks up at the ceiling, then back at me. "What if, um, maybe I . . . uh—"

As he stumbles over his words, his cheeks transforming from pink to scarlet, it hits me.

Oh my gosh. Is Subwayboy about to offer to kiss me?

"Sara Lin!"

We jolt away from each other, Oliver's back hitting the desk as my brain registers the new voice in the room. In seconds, we're scrambling to our feet just in time to see Patrick halt in the doorway. He's panting hard, like he ran up the stairs and down the hall to find us. His cheeks are flushed, but his blue eyes flash with determination.

Great, he's probably here to gloat about how he's won the bet. Now I'm going to have to resign from newspaper and—

"I can't let you lose this bet," Patrick breathes, interrupting my thought spiral.

I blink. "What?"

He steps toward me. Oliver reels back, probably just as confused as I am, taking him in.

And then Patrick's close, closer than we've ever been before, and his good hand comes to carefully cup my face as he gazes into my eyes. I'd almost forgotten how blue they are. A light-blue sky on a clear day. I wonder if he's going to bend down and whisper something into my ear so Oliver can't hear, but that's not what happens.

He leans in, and before I can process what he's doing—his lips come down to meet mine.

My eyes widen. Patrick is kissing me.

Patrick. Is. Kissing. *Me.*

My first kiss.

Oh gosh! His lips are soft, a gentle pressure on mine, but confident and sure. All my thoughts narrow into this singular moment: my lips on his and his on mine, and then my world tips over, a dreamy shimmer blurring my vision as my heart gallops in my chest. A light thrill zigzags up my spine, because this is it.

The final kiss bet.

And Patrick's made sure I've won.

ACKNOWLEDGMENTS

Thank you to WEBTOON, Deanna McFadden, Fiona Simpson, and Ingrid Ochoa for the opportunity to step into the delightful world of *The Kiss Bet.* I loved uncovering captivating ways to bring these characters to life through this novelization. Thank you to my agent, Suzie Townsend, and the team at New Leaf Literary for all that you do. And to my friends and family, thank you for your continuous support.

ABOUT THE AUTHORS

Farrah Penn is an author based in Los Angeles. She graduated from the University of North Texas with a degree in creative writing, and her published works include *Cancelled*, *Twelve Steps to Normal*, and *Right Where We Belong*.

Ingrid Ochoa is a Mexican writer, illustrator, cat owner, and full time WEBTOON creator. Her most famous work is the number one WEBTOON series in the universe (of her mom's heart) called *The Kiss Bet*.

Don't miss *The Kiss Bet* graphic novels!

AVAILABLE NOW